FOREVER FALL

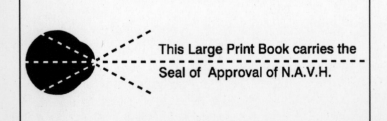

This Large Print Book carries the
Seal of Approval of N.A.V.H.

A HAWKS MOUNTAIN NOVEL

FOREVER FALL

ELIZABETH SINCLAIR

THORNDIKE PRESS
A part of Gale, Cengage Learning

GALE
CENGAGE Learning®

Detroit • New York • San Francisco • New Haven, Conn • Waterville, Maine • London

GALE
CENGAGE Learning®

Sinclair,
Elizabeth

LIBRARY OF CONGRESS CATALOGING-IN-PUBLICATION DATA

Sinclair, Elizabeth.
    Forever fall / by Elizabeth Sinclair.
       pages cm. — (A Hawks Mountain novel ; #3) (Thorndike Press large print clean reads)
    ISBN-13: 978-1-4104-5609-0 (hardcover)
    ISBN-10: 1-4104-5609-9 (hardcover)
    1. Social workers—Fiction. 2. High school principals—Fiction. 3. Teenage pregnancy—Prevention—Fiction. 4. Parenting—Study and teaching—Fiction. 5. Large type books. I. Title.
    PS3619.I5677F67 2013
    813'.6—dc23   2012045628

Published in 2013 by arrangement with BelleBooks, Inc.

To all the single moms struggling to raise their babies on their own. God bless you all and keep you and your babies safe and secure.

Fall
Hi there!

I'm so glad you could stop back and see my mountain in all its fall finery. It never ceases to amaze me how the good Lord finds time to make His Earth so beautiful with each passing season. This fall He seems to have outdone Himself, dressing up the trees in bright orange, red and yellow. Why, the mountain seems to just glow with all that color.

Fall is definitely in the air. All the signs are there. The men are already starting to talk about the World Series and who's gonna win. The pumpkins are ripening in the fields; the corn is ready to harvest; Bessie has decked out the town square in a rainbow of chrysanthemums; and the smell of burning leaves is perfuming the air. Even though it's only the beginning of September, Sam Watkins reports that he's gonna have a fine pumpkin crop, and the young'uns are already trying to decide what to wear for Halloween. The apple crop seems to be extra fine this year, too, all red and juicy. I've already made a few pies for Becky and Nick, and I think I'll do candied apples for the kids for Halloween. I don't get many trick or treaters up here on the mountain. Only those that their parents don't mind totin' up here in their cars. But I always look forward to the little ones coming by and showing off their costumes.

Lydia Collins says Davy wants to dress up like the huntsman from *Red Riding Hood* and take his pet wolf, Sadie, along with him. Lydia's not too sure that's a good idea. Despite Sadie acting like a big, old, gentle dog with Davy, there's some folks still scared witless of that big wolf.

School starts next week, and Becky says that her new social worker, Amantha (she goes by Mandy) James, will be showing up at the first school board meeting with her idea for cutting down on the teenage pregnancies in town. Should be quite a show. Most of the town's planning on turning out for it. Poor Lucas Michaels, the principal, is gonna have a tangle to sort through. I'm sure if Asa Watkins, the School Superintendent, has any say in it (and I can't feature him not adding his two cents), Mandy is gonna have a fight on her hands.

I hear tell the house that Jonathan Prince fella is building outside of town is finally done, and it's a regular palace from all reports. I can't figure why anyone would want a house that big, unless they were married and had a slew of young'uns to fill it up. But, as I always say, to each his own. He and his family have moved in, and I wish them well.

I guess we all have our reasons for what we do. Some talk about it, others keep it hidden deep inside so only they know about it.

They tell me that the phone company has put up a cell tower on the outskirts of town, so most folks in the valley can use those little phones they carry around with them like a lifeline. Guess it's true, 'cause now, when I go to Keeler's Market, I see people walking up and down the aisles with those things glued to their heads like a third ear. Personally, I still like face-to-face conversations. If I wanted to talk to some gadget, I'd have long heart-to-hearts with my refrigerator. Becky's always tellin' me I need to keep up with times. She might be right. But I sure do love a nice chat over a cup of tea. I can't imagine getting the same warm feeling from talking into some gadget. Besides, you can learn a lot looking at a person eye-to-eye.

Well, it's time for Lydia's radio show, so I best get into the parlor and turn on the radio so I don't miss it. You all can stick around and see what's developing. If it's action you're looking for, I promise, Carson won't disappoint you.

Love,
Granny Jo

CHAPTER 1

"It's simple, Luc, if this woman gets her way, I'll see to it that your contract as principal of Carson High School isn't renewed." Asa Watkins, the Superintendent of Carson High School's Board of Education, folded his hands over his thickening middle, crossed his legs and assumed a self-satisfied demeanor.

For Lucas Michaels, the high school principal, the posh offices of Carson Savings and Loan seemed suddenly stifling. He adjusted his position in the cushy, leather chair. Until this moment, Asa had toyed with Luc, hinting at the consequences of not supporting him in his bid to stop the introduction of baby simulators into the school's family planning classes. Now, the gloves were off, and there was no mistaking the superintendent's intent.

"And exactly how do you plan on doing that? I believe it takes the vote of the entire board to dismiss my contract renewal."

Asa smiled, his expression reminding Luc of a cat that had just finished a big bowl of rich cream. "I'm not without influence on the board. I hold a number of the mortgages in this town." The smile faded into an expression of self-assured arrogance.

It sickened Luc that Asa had no qualms about using his financial hold on the other board members to achieve his goal.

Asa waved his hand in a gesture of dismissal. "They're all lemmings. They follow the leader wherever he chooses to lead them." The look of arrogance intensified. "In this instance, I am the leader, and I do not intend to take them in a direction that will drain funds from the athletic department's budget."

"If your influence is all that great, why not just cut to the chase and talk them out of supporting it?" Luc struggled to keep his absolute distaste for this arrogant, pompous jerk under wraps and not bound across the desk to pop him in the mouth.

Asa's dark brows arched. His beady, gray-eyed gaze bore into Luc. "I don't have to tell you that the people of Carson put great stock in our outstanding record of obtaining athletic scholarships. Why, half of them wouldn't be able to send their kids to college at all without them." His expression grew hard. He leaned forward and glared at Luc over his pristine oak desk. "I intend to run for mayor in the upcoming election, and I don't want my record blackened by wasting money on something as asinine as buying dolls for teenagers to play house with. That said, neither do I want to go down in Carson's history as the man who condoned teenage pregnancy."

Luc flashed him a sardonic grin. "You'd rather it be me who holds that distinction."

In every situation, his military father had told Luc, there is always someone who is expendable. It seemed Luc had been assigned that role. Still, the bad taste that had flooded his mouth about the same time he'd received Asa's summons returned and intensified.

"If I agree to do this. . . ." In an effort to keep his true feelings hidden, Luc casually brushed a piece of lint off the cuff of his navy suit jacket. "Exactly how would you suggest I go about it?"

Asa's smile held an almost fiendish satisfaction. "I'm sure that between now and the board meeting next week, you'll come up with some solid arguments against Ms. James' hare-brained notion of spending bundles of money on her robot dolls."

It would seem that if Luc wanted to keep his job, he didn't have a choice in the matter. Though he hated himself and Asa Watkins for the position in which he found himself, Luc had to consider the consequences of not complying with Asa's demands.

Luc treasured the life he'd made for himself in Carson: the first stable home he'd ever known, good friends, a job he loved. Could he give all that up for the sake of a woman who wanted to introduce some dolls into the curriculum? After all, there were already effective forms of birth control and family planning taught in the school. It wasn't as if he'd be leaving the kids with nothing. Still, he hated buckling in to Asa. However, left with little choice. . . .

Luc forced a smile. "I'll do my best."

Asa's hard expression melted into a satisfied grin. "I knew I could count on you, my boy."

Of course you did, you arrogant jerk. You backed me into a corner and left me no escape route.

Asa stood, signifying an end to their meeting. He extended his hand. Luc stuck his in his pocket. Asa let his hand drop back to his side. "In three weeks, it will be my distinct pleasure to recommend to the board that they renew your contract, pending the outcome of the board meeting, of course."

Luc should have been relieved, but he wasn't. He left the bank and headed for his car. His stride alone told anyone passing him that he was not happy. When people began to give him a wide berth, he decided that, for the most part, his expression must have verified his state of mind. He hated being backed into a corner. It reminded him all too vividly of the times his by-the-book Army general father had done just that to him. Luc had wanted to lash out at Asa and tell him he could put the principal job where the sun didn't shine, but he hadn't. Instead, he'd buckled under.

Why?

Instantly, a vision of his house, his friends and his adopted hometown came into his head. Even though he'd only been here for three years, he loved Carson and the people who lived here. Having led a nomadic life as a child, when Luc moved to Carson, he'd settled down and made friends he wouldn't have to leave behind for the first time in his life. He'd held on to these things with a greed only a man who had grown up following his military father and socialite mother from Army base to Army base, leaving friends behind and acclimating to new schools, could. Giving up his position as principal would mean moving to a new community and starting all over again. He couldn't do that for anyone. He could not give up the only real home he'd ever known. Then again, as his father had been fond of saying every time that young Luc had bristled about moving to a new location . . . *nothing is forever.*

If this old maid social worker had been doing her research, she would know that Carson already taught abstinence in the family planning classes and, at great expense, had installed condom vending machines in all the bathrooms. How could she expect them to spend yet more money on these *robo* babies of hers?

By the time Luc reached his car, he wasn't any happier with Asa, nor with the task he'd given Luc, but he had made a modicum of peace with his own conscience about what he had to do.

I'm dead meat!

Amantha James forced herself not to squirm in the hard, straight-back, oak chair. She raised her gaze to survey the cause of her unrest. Like five hungry vultures sitting on a fence, the Carson School Board studied her from behind the long library table. All but one, the only woman on the board, looked as if they'd already made up their minds, and their decision didn't look promising.

Keep your cool. Don't start jumping to conclusions. You haven't even presented your case yet. Besides, this isn't the first time you've come up against a wall of opposition, nor will it be the last.

Easier said than done, however, considering that, with every loud tick of the school clock behind her, their concentrated gazes shot tiny arrows of doubt into her confidence, deflating it at an alarming rate.

She gathered her courage around her and sat a little taller. She'd be darned if she was going to let five people, who would obviously rather be somewhere else, deter her. Very few causes in her life had carried the importance of this one, and she would see it through to the end. All she had to do was hold on a little while longer.

"So, Bill, I didn't see you in the stands at the game Saturday. Last game of the season. Too bad you missed it." Asa Watkins, president of the Carson Savings and Loan and Superintendent of Schools, addressed the man Mandy had already identified as Bill Keeler, owner of the local supermarket.

From the tone of his voice, Mandy decided that Asa's statement held more of a reprimand than a casual interest in the other man's weekend activities.

Bill shook his head and studied his hands. "Mildred and the girls wanted me to take them to the mall down in Prescott."

Asa raised a brow. "Mildred drives, doesn't she? Why couldn't she go herself?"

The man still kept his face averted from his questioner. "She doesn't take to driving in heavy traffic. Always has me go along to take the wheel."

"Well," Asa said, leaning back in his chair and crossing his hands over his ample middle, "you missed a great game. That Jeb Tanner's some ballplayer."

The man to Asa's other side, the youngest member of the board, leaned into the conversation. Becky Hart, Mandy's superior at the social services office, had told her the young one would be Charles Henderson, the board's accountant.

"His dad told me that he's about certain Jeb will get the athletic scholarship to UCLA." Henderson smiled. "Boy's got some throwing arm on him."

All three men laughed. The skinny man not quite as exuberantly as the rest, almost as if it was expected of him.

18

Mandy sighed to herself. Becky had been right. This town had *sports* tattooed on their brain cells, and Asa Watkins ruled this group with an iron fist. She was going to have to talk herself blue to get past using money from their over-endowed athletic department to fund her project.

"Jeb's an ace quarterback, no doubt about that, and a sure thing for a football scholarship from one of the big schools. I told his father last spring that Jeb's lateral pass would be the key." Asa smiled at his companions, his chest expanding to indicate his part in this potential victory. "When that UCLA scout came to the first game, I just knew from the look on the guy's face that Jeb will have it in the bag. Before the scout left, he indicated he'd be back at the end of the year."

"How many scholarships does that make now?" The speaker this time was a man with a clerical collar and a ruddy face, Reverend Thomas, the minister of the local church.

Asa closed his eyes in thought. When they popped open, he grinned like a cat with a fat mouse in his sights. "Five in all. With Jeb's scholarship added to the total, it'll make it six. I may have to get a bigger trophy case for my office." He laughed and transferred his attention to Mandy. His gaze sent a silent message. *Don't mess with me, lady.*

Mandy met it head on with her own silent challenge. *You don't scare me.*

She looked away. Glancing around the old schoolhouse's library, she wondered when the one absent member of their solemn gathering, the school's principal, would show up. She glanced to the open window which admitted a late fall breeze perfumed with the sweet odor of burning leaves that overrode that unique smell of chalk, paper, books and rubber-soled sneakers that hovered in the air in every school. Forcing calm to her jangled nerves, she inhaled deeply and peered at her watch. Eight thirty. Half an hour late. How much longer would he make them wait?

Appearing composed and confident got harder with each passing moment. Her back hurt from sitting so straight, the hard chair seat had stolen the feeling from her backside almost twenty minutes ago, and her good mood, along with her patience, was dwindling rapidly. Her stomach rumbled in protest of the supper she'd missed to get here on time. She tugged the sleeve of her red plaid suit jacket over the watch face and tried not to show her agitation.

"Mr. Michaels will be here shortly, Ms.

James. You must understand that this meeting made it necessary for him to rearrange his evening to accommodate us." The explanation came from Asa Watkins.

Watkins, a single, fortyish man, who had been keeping a close eye on the height of Mandy's skirt hem, had caught her agitated movements. As unobtrusively as possible, she pulled her skirt lower over her knees and smiled.

"I understand." What she wanted to say and didn't dare was that, having known about the meeting for weeks, she found the principal's tardiness rude and inconsiderate. But why shoot herself in the foot before she'd had the opportunity to present her case?

To keep her mind off her growing irritation with the absent Lucas Michaels, she scanned the five people at the long library table. She tried to guess their voting preference, but a cool, feminine voice interrupted her before she could start.

"While we wait, why don't you fill us in on your proposal, my dear?" Catherine Daniels, the only female member and the town matriarch, drew Mandy's attention. The older woman smiled graciously from beneath a navy, feather-encrusted hat, no doubt custom-designed for her by some exclusive New York City milliner.

She returned Catherine's smile. "If it's all right with the board, I'd rather wait until Mr. Michaels is here, so I don't have to cover everything again."

Just then the door at the rear of the school's small library opened on squeaky hinges. She turned to see a very tall man in a gray business suit, white shirt and a conservative, burgundy tie enter the room, briefcase in hand, his forehead creased in a frown. As he walked slowly to the front of the room, his spit-polished wing-tips clicked rhythmically across the oiled hardwood floor.

Mandy's breath left her lungs in a painful *whoosh*. Oddly enough, she seemed unable to replenish it. For the first time that night, gratitude for the hard, uncomfortable chair seeped into her. Without it, she wasn't at all sure her legs would have held her body weight.

With his dark, good looks, the principal of Carson High School could have just stepped off the cover of *Hunk of the Month*. Mandy had seen him around town and had to admit that, like most of the single women and the high school girls, Lucas Michaels demanded closer female scrutiny. And if she wanted to be totally honest, she'd taken her share of glances at the handsome principal, and maybe even fantasized about him a bit. However, she had no plans to become another notch on his bedpost or, for that matter, any other man's.

"Ah, Luc, finally. *Now,* we can get started." Asa's greeting interrupted her musings. She noted that his tone held a hint of rebuke, which seemed to roll off Lucas Michaels like rain off a greased windowpane.

Mandy gave herself a severe mental shake. Ogling the principal wouldn't sell the board on her idea to cut down the alarming rate of teenage pregnancy in their small town. If the determined set of Lucas Michaels' expression meant anything, convincing him wouldn't be an easy task. But, if it meant saving one teen from experiencing the life Mandy had lived as the illegitimate daughter of an embittered, single, alcoholic mother, she'd face the devil himself.

She issued a silent affirmation to his stiff profile and to her own psyche. *I am not a loser, Mr. Michaels.*

Being ordered to do anything went against Luc's grain. The visit he'd made to Asa's office days before still had the power to rankle him. Making no apologies for his tardy arrival, he took a seat in the unoccupied chair facing the board table. Putting his briefcase on his lap, he clicked it open, extracted a fat, manila file folder, closed the lid, and then placed the leather case beside him on the floor.

He deliberately avoided looking to his left at the woman who had urged Asa to call this meeting, a device Luc often used on a student to unsettle them enough to get to the bottom of a matter.

Luc crossed his legs and folded his hands on the file, then smiled at the board members. "Good evening."

"Good evening, Luc. Thank you for coming." Asa fumbled through some papers, never really meeting him eye to eye.

Was he feeling a bit guilty about what he had planned for this evening? Luc laughed inwardly. He couldn't envision Asa feeling one ounce of guilt for anything he'd ever done in his life.

Asa pounded the table with his gavel, and all conversation in the room ceased instantly. "Now that we're all here, shall we get started?"

Luc made no reply. No sense pretending courtesy had anything to do with his appearance here tonight. He'd made Asa fully aware that he hated what they were doing. The other board members nodded in Luc's direction.

He could hear the woman stirring in her chair.

He smiled inwardly.

Lack of composure would cause her to make a slipshod presentation, giving the board good reason to turn her down. With any luck, he might not have to play the heavy in this. Being cast in the role of the bad guy was not new ground to Luc. This wasn't the first time Asa had used Luc and relied on him to not only side with Asa, but also to turn the tide in their favor. This was, however, the first time Luc's job depended on it, and the first time his conscience really bothered him.

He hated the control Asa exerted over him, but looked at it as a part of the job, even if, in his own mind, he knew it to be out and out blackmail. There was a pecking order in all occupations, and unless you occupied the top seat, you learned to take orders without question. His father had ingrained that in Luc early in his childhood.

Asa Watkins interrupted Luc's thoughts. "Ms. James, I don't believe you've met Lucas Michaels, our principal."

"Mr. Michaels." Though somewhat stiff, her voice held a very pleasing quality, the kind a man could listen to for hours and not tire of.

Continuing with his calculated plan to unnerve her, while keeping his gaze fixed on Asa, Luc merely nodded in the direction of the feminine voice.

"If you're ready, Ms. James, you can get us started by filling us in on your proposal." Asa smiled toward the source of an enticing perfume drifting in Luc's direction. Flowery, soft. Not overpowering. Subtly suggestive.

Calculated, he added with a brisk shake to his imagination. If she thought she could make points with her feminine wiles, then she was sadly mistaken. He'd seen his mother do this many times when trying to get his father to cave on some issue.

"Thank you, Mr. Watkins." The raspy quality of her voice raked over Luc's nerve endings, bringing tiny pin-pricks of pleasure to his senses.

A bedroom voice.

"As you all know, I'm the new social worker assigned to the Carson office. I've been here for three months, and in that time I've come across some alarming statistics about the rising number of teenage pregnancies, mostly concerning unwed, high school students. In the information I will give you tonight, I've noted the precise percentage and relevant data that will speak for itself."

Reverend Thomas emitted a loud hiss of

26

air. Mandy couldn't ascertain if it indicated his agreement with her statement or his displeasure with the reality of the facts.

"I have done some research into preventatives and, if you'll allow me, I'll pass out some information I have gathered for a possible answer."

Asa nodded his permission.

From his peripheral vision, Luc had a shadowy image of the woman standing, carrying a pile of papers, and walking to the table, where she passed out several sheets to each board member. Then she turned to Luc, papers in her outstretched hand.

He looked up into the face of one of the most gorgeous women he had ever seen. His breath snagged. So this was Amantha James. So much for the old-maid-social-worker image.

Instantly, he recalled having seen her several times at the school. He'd had no idea why she was there, and just assumed she had a sibling or a child enrolled and had come to see them for some reason. What he did recall is the astounding effect she'd had on his libido. It had taken days to erase her image from his mind.

"Mr. Michaels?"

Dragging his attention from her mesmerizing, coffee brown eyes and deeply implanted dimples, he accepted the papers. "Thank you."

Was that squeaky voice his? He cleared his throat and gazed at the paper clutched in his hand. The words blurred. Feeling as if he'd been kicked by a horse, he drew in a labored breath.

After blinking several times, he was finally able to make out the words at the top of the page, *Baby Simulators.*

"Robo babies," he mumbled under his breath.

"Mr. Michaels, until I've explained, please don't make any snap judgments." Her voice betrayed a hint of impatience.

Keeping his gaze trained on the paper, he shrugged. "Be my guest."

This was ridiculous. Was he going to let some ego-driven social worker rattle him? He'd never felt so completely off track in his life, at least not since his last bout with his father. Luc made it a point to keep his footing in any and all situations. Not doing so meant stepping into uncharted territory, and Luc never ventured into anything of which he wasn't fully aware. He mustn't forget that it was his plan to rattle *her*. He sat straighter, marshaling his forces for his attack.

"The baby simulator is a device to aid in

family planning for teens. As you can see from the pictures in the flyers I just gave you, it resembles a real baby in every way, appearance, weight and temperament, as well as being anatomically correct."

"Do you mean to say these . . . *robo* babies have . . . well, that they. . . ." Having been raised around a prissy mother who *just didn't talk about such things in mixed company,* he couldn't force the words to emerge. Luc glanced up to see several of the board members hiding a smile behind their hands. Luc felt like a complete fool, an adolescent too embarrassed to discuss sex in clinical terms.

"Yes, Mr. Michaels. As I said, they are anatomically correct," the James woman said, a smile playing around her luscious mouth. He quickly averted his gaze. "The manufacturer made certain that the simulators would resemble real babies in *every* way. And I can safely say that I doubt if these characteristics will not come as a shock to any of the teens who will participate in this project." The hint of laughter in her voice told him she obviously found his discomfort with the subject amusing.

"*If* it is approved," Luc added pointedly.

"*If* it is approved." A small concession on her part. She smiled at the board.

"Thank you," he said, stiffly.

"I don't understand how these simulators are going to prevent pregnancies." Catherine Daniels studied the paper in her hand and then glanced at Mandy. "Wouldn't this be akin to letting the students play with dolls?"

"No. It's much more complicated than that. I might add here that we must think of them as babies and not dolls to get the potential caregivers to think of them in those terms as well.

"Now, if you look closely at the picture on page four of the information, you'll see that each baby is equipped with a care monitor implanted in its back. This allows the teacher or project supervisor to monitor the type and frequency of care given the baby." Mandy waited for the board to review the information.

"But why couldn't we just continue to use the sack of flour or an egg? It'd be a whole lot cheaper, and I'm sure Bill would appreciate the business." Reverend Thomas smiled and leaned his arms on the unopened folder resting on the table in front of him.

Laughter bubbled up around the table and then died.

"The simulator has some distinctly human-like qualities that the egg and the flour sack don't. The baby is programmed to cry at unpredictable intervals, twenty-four hours a day, just as a real baby will. Its disposition can also be adjusted from mild to very cranky. The head must be supported, and the baby cannot be allowed to cry too long, fall or be treated roughly. If any of these events occur, then that registers on the care monitor, and the caregiver earns demerits." Mandy resumed her seat and waited for more questions.

"As amazing as this technology is, I don't understand how these *robo* babies are going to cut the number of teenage pregnancies, Ms. James?" Mandy tried hard to overlook the hint of suppressed amusement coloring Lucas Michaels' voice.

Taking a deep breath and ignoring the muffled agreement from the board, Mandy faced the principal. She set her expression to reflect the serious nature of her subject, rather than her irritation with him. "Each baby comes with a key to be inserted and held in a slot in the back of the simulator, then anywhere from one to thirty minutes will elapse before the baby stops crying. This is to show the caregiver that food or diaper changes are not always the reason a baby cries."

"I still don't see how this can be a deterrent. The caregiver can simply leave the key with a parent and go about their normal social life." Luc knew firsthand about how easy it was to hand off responsibility and care for a child to someone else, even a robot child.

She addressed her explanation to the entire board. "Not in this case, which is part of the beauty of this simulator. The key is attached to the caregiver's wrist permanently for the duration of the project, much like a hospital bracelet is attached. He or she is the only one who can minister to the baby. Therefore, if the caregiver leaves the house for whatever reason, the baby must go along. If he or she doesn't take the baby, and it cries in her absence, the baby will cry until the battery runs down, and the caregiver will get demerits for neglect." She turned toward Luc.

"Think of yourself as a teenager with a social life, Mr. Michaels. Taking this baby with you everywhere can be a real drag. Studies have shown that after caring for this baby for as little as a week, many teens have decided to wait to become parents, and some have even opted out of parenthood altogether."

A grunt and a nod of agreement came from Bill Keeler. The board stared at Mandy in rapt attention. Catherine Daniels concentrated on the information sheets.

Seemingly encouraged by their silence, Mandy went on. "The inconvenience of caring for the baby and the restrictions it puts on the social lives of the teen parent can be very effective arguments for not having children. Rather than having an adult preach to them about the responsibilities that go along with being a parent, they'll actually live with it every day for a prescribed period of time. Of course, classroom re-enforcement will be given also, but the hands-on experience will validate what they learn in the classroom, bringing it home as no amount of preaching could."

Luc realized that this woman had obviously done her homework. Tripping her up was not going to be easy, if they could at all. Her arguments held well-thought-out logic. How could he argue with logic? New respect for Ms. James surged through him. This was not some empty-headed twit that Asa could snowball.

He had to find a crack in her argument that would allow the board to vote this suggestion into the ground. And he knew just where to look for that flaw.

"Let's look at the bottom line here, Ms. James. What will it cost the school to get this program started?" Luc leaned back in his chair.

Out of the corner of his eye, he noted that Charles Henderson, ever the accountant, had readied his pencil to write down the figures he expected to be forthcoming from Mandy.

If the board had to take money from their precious, inflated athletic department budget to finance this scheme of Ms. James', there would be no baby simulators coming into Carson High. And having access to the budget and its allotment, Luc knew Asa had been right in that respect anyway. He could see no other venue from which to get the money. He glanced at Mandy and waited for her bottom line.

"To be effective, the program should start out fully equipped to provide at least half of the students in the class with a simulator to care for during the first phase of the project. The simulators would then go to the other half of the class for the second phase." She took a deep breath. Her next bit of information would either make or break the entire project. "Please look at the amount I'm about to quote as an investment in your youth and in the future of this community." She named the price per baby.

With a sinking heart, she watched their collected faces register everything from shock to absolute rejection — everyone except Catherine Daniels. Was she going for the idea, or did money mean so little to her?

Charles Henderson's accountant's mind clicked in. "And exactly where would you suggest we access the funds to buy these . . . baby simulators?"

This was the one stumbling block in her plan. She had no idea if the school had money for unbudgeted purchases, but she was aware that they had a huge athletic budget. However, Becky Hart had advised her strongly to allow the board to find their funds without any prompting from her.

Mandy shook her head. "I'm sure you can answer that better than I can. Since I'm not privy to the school's operating budget. . . ."

Asa Watkins, who had been ominously quiet until now, looked pointedly at Luc. "Perhaps we should get some input on this point from Luc."

Luc stared at Asa for a long time, hearing the words the superintendent had said as Luc had left Asa's office the week before.

It's simple, Luc. If this woman gets her way, I'll see to it that your contract as principal isn't renewed.

Luc had gotten the message loud and clear. If this proposal went through, the only logical place to get the funding was to cut back the athletic department's lion's share of the school budget. Support anything that would jeopardize the athletic scholarships, and he'd be history in Carson.

Though it grated against his better judgment, Luc was not about to give up the life he had so painstakingly established and start all over.

He straightened in his chair and looked directly at Asa. "Well, the athletic budget has already been strained by adding a new chemistry teacher to the faculty. I really don't think —"

Becky had warned her, but Mandy still couldn't believe her ears. "The athletic budget?" Mandy fought to control her anger. "When did sports become more important than the welfare of your children?"

Lucas Michaels glared at her. "That's not the case at all. If you'll allow me to finish, Ms. James." Mandy leaned back in her chair, her arms crossed over her chest, her expression clearly exposing her efforts to control her temper. "The welfare of our children is, of course, uppermost in our minds. However, the athletic scholarships that our students earn are immeasurably helpful in getting them into colleges that would otherwise be financially out of the question for them. It occurs to me that we are already doing a sufficient amount of preventative teaching by supplying condoms and teaching abstinence —"

"Abstinence?" That was the last straw. Mandy jumped to her feet and faced him. "Abstinence, Mr. Michaels? You want to preach abstinence to a bunch of teenagers with raging hormones? Hormones they've just discovered and are chomping at the bit to experiment with?"

"Aren't you being just a bit over-reactive?"

Mandy couldn't believe this. They might as well put a bottle of whiskey in front of a confirmed alcoholic and say *don't touch.* If it wasn't so sad, she'd have laughed out loud at the absurdity of his statement. What was wrong with him? Didn't he care about these kids?

As far as abstinence went, who was Michaels kidding? What could a man with his good looks and obvious charm know about abstinence? He probably had women coming and going from his bed with all the regularity of planes at Charleston's Yeager Airport.

That the board would put sports before the welfare of a child enraged her. The collective lack of logic and caring for their own children displayed by the board and the

37

school principal severed her already strained composure, along with any attempt at caution.

"And, of course, you know all about abstinence, right, Mr. Michaels?" Sarcasm dripped from Mandy's words.

A collective gasp rose from the board table.

Asa smiled.

Instantly, Mandy knew she'd overstepped her bounds and may have made a fatal mistake in attacking Luc, but her frustration level had imprudently pushed the words from her lips before she'd been able to stop them.

Slowly, Luc uncrossed his legs, then targeted her with a dark, censoring glare. "As a matter of fact, Ms. James, I grew up in all-boys military schools, which left little opportunity for anything but abstinence." His gaze grew colder. "So, to answer your question, yes, I do know about abstinence."

"I'm very sorry. That remark was beyond rude, Mr. Michaels. I can only blame it on my passion for the subject."

Luc raised an eyebrow and nodded. "Passion, huh?" The corner of his mouth quirked up in a suggestive half smile, then immediately relaxed into a firmly set expression of censure.

Passion? She didn't like the way he'd said that or that smile.

Before Mandy could say anything, Catherine Daniels intervened. "Please, let's leave personalities out of this." She glanced at her fellow board members and favored them with a smile. "If the board will allow me, I have a suggestion that might settle this whole matter."

The members looked at each other and then back to her. Collectively, they shrugged, then nodded in agreement to let her voice her plan.

"I think we should give the babies . . . a test drive." She looked at Mandy. "Do you have one of these simulators available?"

A glow of hope rose in Mandy. Had she found a sympathetic ear in Catherine? "I don't have one with me, but I know we can borrow one from the company. They assured me that because of the huge investment, testing the system is quite common."

Catherine smiled. "Good." She leaned back in her chair and extracted a white handkerchief from her purse. Carefully, she used the handkerchief to brush a spot of dirt from the lapel of her pristine navy suit.

"Can we get on with it, Catherine?" Bill Keeler obviously had grown impatient with the entire process. Mandy had to agree with him. "I promised Mildred I'd be home by ten."

"Patience, Bill, patience. I want to get everything straight in my mind before I present it. This young woman's suggestion has merit, and I think we need to give it more than cursory consideration. As for you hurrying home, I'm sure you'd rather be anywhere but 47 Elm Street, so don't use that as an excuse to get to Hannigan's Bar for your nightcap."

Bill sat back in his chair, his cheeks glowing bright red.

Mandy hid a smile and grasped at the thread of hope Catherine had thrown her. Maybe she hadn't ruined everything with her outburst.

Asa looked around at his fellow board members. "Let's give Catherine a chance to explain what she has in mind." His tone held reluctant resignation rather than enthusiasm.

"We seem to have two distinctly different viewpoints here, neither of which any of us are equipped to make judgments on. My suggestion is that the baby simulator be put to the test in a real family setting. Once that's completed, we can use the findings to make an informed decision."

Reverend John Thomas leaned forward to

address Catherine. "And exactly who would you suggest do this testing, Catherine? All the board members, having already experienced the dubious joys of parenthood, would know what to expect. Thus making us the guinea pigs would prove nothing. And I'd like to go on record as saying that until the board makes a decision, I strongly object to bringing anyone in from the outside."

"Exactly, John." Catherine smiled sweetly and turned back to Mandy and Luc. "That's why we need a couple who can keep this discreetly confidential and who have no parenting experience. The obvious choices for the test are Ms. James and Mr. Michaels."

CHAPTER 2

Luc was sure he should be picking his jaw up off the school library's floor. He looked in horror at the stunned school board, then at the stricken expression on Amantha James' face. Well, at least he wasn't the only one who felt as if he'd just taken a punch to his gut.

Could Catherine Daniels mean what it sounded like she meant? Did she expect him to set up housekeeping with this social worker to oversee the testing of the *robo* baby?

Reverend Thomas was the first to find his voice. "Catherine? Ah . . . if you don't mind my saying so, this sounds most improper."

"I should say so," Asa chimed in. "What would the community think if they found out their school board was involved in something like this?"

Catherine Daniels smiled, as if enjoying being able to disrupt the stoic calm of this group of sports-biased thinkers. "If you'll give me a moment, gentlemen, I intend to expand on my statement, so you can put away your holier-than-thou tone. I can assure you, there is nothing improper about what I am about to propose."

She settled herself more comfortably in her chair, folded her hands in front of her on the table, and then zeroed in on Luc and Mandy. "I know a teenage girl who is very much enamored with the idea of having a child. She's only fifteen and has just about driven her parents to the brink of mental breakdown with her misdirected desire to become a mother. I'm sure they would cooperate and agree to anything that might deter her from these inconceivable thoughts."

Still not understanding why the problems of a teenager involved him and Mandy James, Luc leaned forward. "And Ms. James and I are a part of this in what way?"

Luc watched a smile transform Catherine's composed face into a semblance of the classic Renoir beauty she must have been as a young girl. "You and Ms. James will get to play parents to this girl for two weeks . . . discreetly, of course. At the end of that time, I will ask the girl if she's ready to give up her dreams of teenage motherhood. If she

43

is, then the board will reconsider Ms. James' request. If not, then the subject of introducing the infant simulators at Carson High School will be dropped."

Catherine cast a sidelong glance at her fellow board members. "Agreed?" Some hesitated, but they all eventually nodded in the affirmative, Asa being the last, his expression clearly broadcasting his reluctance. "Good. Due to the sensitive nature of the situation, I propose that the board leave the details to me, Ms. James and Luc, and that this test be conducted with the utmost discretion." Catherine looked to Mandy. "Well, Ms. James?"

Mandy hesitated to answer. Living with the insufferable Mr. Lucas for two weeks? Could she do it without doing him bodily harm? Did she have a choice? Finally, she nodded. "Yes. I'll do the test."

Luc sighed. He was hoping Ms. James would say no. Since she hadn't, that left him holding the proverbial bag.

The glaring stare that Asa leveled on him told Luc, without saying the words, that he'd better see to it that the test concluded in Asa's favor. If not, then Luc would be out on his ear, pounding the pavement, looking for a new job and probably without references. He looked back to find Catherine's gaze centered intently on him, along with those of the board and that of Ms. James.

Luc sighed. "Very well."

The following morning, Luc still hadn't digested entirely what he'd agreed to. Despite having a pile of work still on his desk, and even though he'd specifically come in early to get caught up, he had swiveled his chair toward the window. He stared blankly out over the deserted athletic field, still convinced the location of the principal's office had been carefully calculated by the board to remind him of his priorities, and thought about this test Catherine had devised.

The worst of it was, he could see the sound thinking behind Mandy's request, and, truth be known, he wouldn't have minded seeing her get board approval, if it hadn't meant losing his job in the bargain.

He'd gone up against his father too many times not to know that the one with rank held the power. And Asa Watkins, horse's ass that he was, held both. Yes, Catherine had a huge voice on the board, but Asa was not shy about using any means he could to get his way. Asa's compliance with Catherine's test constituted no more than lip

45

service, and he would, if Mandy won, find a way to make his famous "end play" and take home the victory anyway. Mandy didn't know it, but, if Asa Watkins had anything to do with it, her simulators would never see the inside of Carson High School — no matter how this so-called test concluded.

Luc slammed his hand on the arm of his desk chair. He hated this. Hated everything about the entire mess. Then, he calmed himself. He should wait to see exactly what Catherine had in mind before he went off the deep end. Maybe this wouldn't be the catastrophe he envisioned. After all, how bad could it be being trapped in the constant company of a beautiful woman for two weeks?

How bad indeed?

His head swirled with visions of her lips, her curvy legs, her soft bedroom voice and that perfume that reached out and wrapped itself around his . . .

Sweat immediately beaded his forehead. He pulled a folded white handkerchief from his jacket's breast pocket, then swiped his brow dry. If his physical reaction was anything to go by, then Chinese water torture would be a breeze in comparison to two weeks with Mandy James.

What in God's name have you gotten your-

self into?

The phone jingled. He swiveled back to face the desk, then lifted the receiver from the cradle. Clearing his throat of sexual frustration, he spoke calmly into the mouthpiece. "Hello."

"Lucas. Catherine Daniels here."

"Catherine, what can I do for you?" He fought to hide the apprehension in his voice.

"You can meet Ms. James and me at the Lodge on the Lake today at one o'clock for lunch."

Luc hesitated before answering. He wasn't at all sure he was ready to meet Ms. James anywhere, at any time, again soon. "Am I to assume this is in connection with the preposterous test you suggested last night at the board meeting?"

"You may." Her initially friendly tone had turned crisp. "I will expect you at one o'clock, Lucas. Don't be late." The phone went dead.

He stared at the receiver for a time, wondering if he could arrange a quiet, painless suicide before one o'clock.

"Mr. Michaels?"

What now? He quickly hung up the phone and turned to face his secretary. "Yes, Barbara?"

"The Tanner boy is here."

"Wait a minute or two, then send him in."

The door closed, and Luc immediately pushed aside his private problems and directed his attention to the file laying open on his desk.

Jeb Tanner's grades had dropped significantly last year and didn't look much better so far this year, and Luc wanted to know why. Jeb aspired to go to UCLA to get his degree and teach. If he kept letting his grades slip, his chances of winning any kind of scholarship, or even being admitted, would seriously diminish — no matter how good his prowess on an athletic field.

The door opened, and a handsome, young blond boy stepped through it, his sky-blue eyes confident and calm. He wore a red sweatshirt with the words *Go Cougars!* across the front and his football squad number below it in white.

"Hello, Jeb." Luc smiled warmly and motioned toward the chair across from him. "Please, sit down."

Jeb slid into the chair, then sprawled his legs out in front of him. "What's up, Mr. M?"

Jeb's relaxed attitude helped renew the faith Luc had in himself as a fair and just administrator. Luc picked up a pencil and tapped the file. "Your teachers tell me your grades took a big drop at the end of your junior year. And, it seems to be a trend that you've continued this year. Is there anything wrong?" Luc adjusted his voice to what he thought of as his *student tone,* one he reserved for dealing with the kids in his school — firm, but friendly.

Had Mandy James heard him now, she would never believe it was the same stern-faced, inflexible man she'd confronted the evening before. He drew a very sharp line between student and adult in his approach, keeping his tone of the night before strictly for dealing with parents and the board of education. That same voice was the one he'd been confronted with on many occasions from his father and the military school superintendents.

A rebellious young man, Luc had been called before the principal many times during his school years, and he'd promised himself that he would not treat any child who came before him like a piece of disposable furniture, without feelings or thoughts. Contrary to Ms. James' assertion of the night before, he did care a great deal about the students in this school. He treated them like thinking human beings with a right to their opinions and emotions, and he liked to think they all respected and liked him for that.

"No, sir, there's nothing wrong."

"The classwork, is it too difficult for you? If it is, we can arrange for extra help."

Jeb shook his head. "No, sir."

"If there's nothing wrong, and the work is not too difficult, then to what do you attribute your grade average drop?" Jeb didn't answer, just continued to stare at Luc. Maybe a different approach. "This is your senior year. If your marks aren't higher this year, then you may be endangering your chances of getting into UCLA."

A smile lit Jeb's face. "No worry there, Mr. Watkins told my dad I'm a shoo-in for the football scholarship."

"He did? When did this happen?" Luc felt a ball of anger forming in the pit of his stomach. Asa had no right getting the boy's hopes up for something that could very well fall through.

"Last fall, after the UCLA scout was here."

Luc's nerves tightened at the boy's words. Jeb was a bright, intelligent young man, with unlimited potential. He was also the star quarterback of the football team, and while his athletic ability could get him into UCLA, if he didn't maintain a 2.5 GPA, he'd miss out on both the scholarship and the degree he wanted. Right now, he was hovering at 2.8, and one bad midterm grade could pull him down. The worst of it was that Luc knew Jeb was capable of much better work.

It would probably take Luc the remainder of the morning to explain to Jeb why he needed more than just a passable grade and an athletic scholarship to establish a lifetime career. In the end, his parents would no doubt come in and tell Luc to mind his own business. However, Luc felt a responsibility to his kids that superseded the threat of parental confrontation.

Since Jeb had already known about the potential scholarship, and his grades so far this year didn't show improvement, Luc wondered if something else had caused it, like girl problems. If that was so, Jeb wouldn't be the first student Luc had counseled through a romantic breakup. But right now, he just couldn't face that prospect.

Quite unexpectedly, he found himself looking forward to lunch with Mandy James and Catherine Daniels.

Driving to the exclusive Lodge on the Lake restaurant, Mandy felt sure she could win

51

this little test, hands down. After all, a teenager with raging hormones wanted to date and have fun, not be tied down with a baby. Teens invariably went into this arrangement thinking it would be nothing more than an instant replay of the time they played with dolls, and when they tired of the limitations of parenthood, there was always Mom to take up the slack, while the teen went off and had fun with friends.

Usually, very little time passed before they realized that parenting involved a good deal more than dressing the baby, cooing at it periodically and, when it represented a complication to their social lives, dismissing it completely or handing it off to Mom. Mandy had only to allow this girl to experience the *joys* of motherhood, and the overeager teen would soon be shelving the idea until further notice.

As for the idea of abstinence that Luc mentioned, she'd never heard such utter nonsense. Take two healthy adolescents, throw them together, and they will inevitably gravitate naturally to dark, secret places, back seats of cars and sexual experimentation. And they do it without a single thought for the consequences, either to their health or that a child could result from their pleasure, and that the child could suffer immeasurably from the parents' transgression. That was something of which Mandy had firsthand knowledge.

Confidence filling her, Mandy swung her car onto the paved drive and followed its landscaped curves to the ornate portico entrance of the picturesque restaurant. Grabbing her purse from the seat, she waited for the valet to open the door, then handed him her keys and climbed out. She smoothed the wrinkles from her beige skirt and headed toward the wide front steps.

However, as confident as she felt, the closer she got to the front door, the more her stomach flipped. Facing Catherine Daniels didn't make her uneasy. Facing the man who had inexplicably haunted her dreams last night, on the other hand, rattled her more than she cared to admit.

Luc spotted Mandy approaching across the crowded dining room before she saw him. Eager to have this over with, he'd arrived early for the meeting with Catherine and Mandy. He'd strategically selected a table facing the door, but overlooking the large lake at the base of the hill on which the restaurant perched. He'd always enjoyed the view of the lake. As for facing the door, he'd learned a long time ago to cover his blind side. Back then, his blind side had been his quick-to-anger father, but right now, it was Mandy James.

Now that he saw her again, he was glad he had time to harness his libido before she reached the table.

The imposing, tuxedo-clad *maître d'* led her across the room. Her hips swayed gracefully with each step she took, making her beige skirt shift softly from side to side, caressing her hips, her obscenely long, curvy legs and her thighs.

Sweat beaded Luc's forehead.

Beneath her whiskey-colored blouse, her breasts moved in rhythm with her hips, making his mouth go dry and his breathing falter. Her long, straight, auburn hair swayed seductively around her face and shoulders. When she spotted him, she tossed the shiny tresses back over one shoulder in a gesture that smacked strongly of challenge.

Loosening the tie that suddenly seemed to be restricting his air passage, he sat straighter in his chair. As casually as he could, he lifted his water goblet and sipped the icy contents, relishing the rush of coolness on his desert-dry throat.

If he was going to have to spend two weeks in close proximity to the intoxicating

Mandy James, he'd have to get himself under control. And, he'd better start now. Setting the goblet back on the snowy white linen tablecloth, he dragged himself to his feet, his napkin held casually, but strategically, in front of him.

"Ms. James," he drawled, trying to sound nonchalant around a smile he hoped welcomed her, but revealed nothing of the turmoil going on inside him.

"Mr. Michaels." Mandy glanced at him, flashed a tentative smile, and then quickly looked away.

Lord, but the man could make a woman's toes curl with a just a glance from those dangerously dark eyes of his.

The waiter held Mandy's chair while she took her seat, then he withdrew.

Luc resumed his own seat and replaced his napkin across his lap. "Catherine called to say she'd be a few minutes late, but for us to order without her."

Mandy nodded, trying to ignore the shiver that passed down her body at the caress of his deep, throaty voice. She doubted she could get a crumb to pass down her tight throat. "I'm not really hungry. If it's okay with you, why don't we wait for Catherine?"

Luc turned to the waiting *maître d'*, accepted the leather bound menus from him, then placed them within easy reach at the table's edge. "We'll wait for Mrs. Daniels."

"Very good, sir." The *maître d'* bowed and stepped aside to allow the hovering waiter access to the table.

"Perhaps some wine while you wait?" The waiter looked from one to the other and offered Luc the wine list.

Luc looked pointedly at Mandy. She shook her head. An alcoholic stimulant was the last thing she needed singing through her veins right now. She never did well with alcohol under the best of circumstances, and Luc was enough stimulant for any red-blooded woman. "Ice tea, please, with lemon."

"Make that two," Luc said.

The waiter bowed again, took the wine lists from Luc and then left them alone.

Mandy fidgeted with her silverware, lining the ends of the handles up perfectly with the horizontal weave in the tablecloth. Anything to avoid direct eye contact with Luc. Annoyed that just being in his presence should have such a strong effect on her, she checked the door, praying Catherine would magically appear.

He broke the strained silence first. "Ms. James —"

She glanced back at him. "Mandy, please.

If we're going to be living together for two weeks, the formalities seem silly." Saying it out loud sent a shiver of — of what? Surely that hadn't been pleasure.

He gave an almost imperceptible nod, his striking dark gaze boring into her. "Very well, Mandy. And please call me Luc. However, I think your assumption about us living together is a bit premature."

Mandy raised an eyebrow. "Oh? I thought that decision had already been made at the board meeting last night." Was he backing out? Her heart dropped. Without him and the test, her chances of getting the simulators into the high school lessened considerably. But was that the only reason? "If you don't intend to agree to the test, then why are you here?"

"I didn't say I wouldn't take part in the test. Let's just say I came to check out . . . the, uh, possibilities."

Despite the way she bristled at the innuendo in his words, the sound of his velvety, deep voice seemed to reach out and touch her in places she hadn't had touched in a very long time. Silently, she sent up a little prayer for an epidemic of laryngitis to strike the small hamlet of Carson for the next two weeks, and Luc in particular.

She sucked in a full breath of air.

57

"Are you all right?"

No, she was far from all right. Her stomach felt bottomless. Like she was riding a roller coaster, and the car had just plunged into one of those death-defying loop de loops.

Quickly, she nodded and averted her eyes. "I'm fine." She took another deep breath to steady herself. "Still catching my breath. Mrs. Daniel's call came at the last minute, and I had to rush through some things before coming here."

Amazed that, when her insides felt like quivering gelatin, her voice sounded so steady, she looked gratefully at the waiter, who had appeared as if by magic at their side. He placed two glasses of ice tea on the table, gave a slight bow, and then left them alone again.

Perhaps if they talked business instead of just sitting here and. . . . "So, Luc, I take it you don't think much of this plan that Mrs. Daniel's has proposed."

"I think we need to wait and see exactly what she has in mind before either of us jumps to any conclusions about it." With his forefinger, he drew small circles in the moisture on the side of his glass. "Two weeks sounds like a snap in time, but this could be a very long snap. I hope you're prepared to make the investment, mentally and. . . ."

He paused. His gaze swept Mandy's face. Had he been about to add *physically*? Then it suddenly occurred to her what he was trying to do — unnerve her. Well, it wasn't going to work. She'd come up against men who were much more subtle about it than Lucas Michaels.

Mandy sat straighter. "Exactly what are you suggesting?"

Luc looked directly at her, his expression all innocence. "What exactly do you think I'm suggesting, Ms. James?"

Mandy felt her face redden. His veiled insinuation sent a pleasurable shiver up her spine. Quickly, she shifted her gaze out the window, but even without looking at him, her awareness of the man studying her so intently heightened.

"Ah, you're both here. Wonderful." Saved by the bell.

Not having realized the degree of tension gripping his body since Mandy sat down, Luc was surprised when he found himself relaxing with Catherine Daniels' arrival.

He stood and smiled at her. "Hello, Catherine."

As usual, the town's matriarch carried herself with understated grace, quietly in charge, yet unmindful and casually accepting of her status in a way that, rather than repel them, beckoned people to approach her. Luc had always admired that in her. Perfectly coiffed, not a snow-white hair ventured from her chic hairdo. Her impeccable, burgundy silk dress needed no designer monograms to tell anyone it had come with an expensive price tag, probably one of a kind.

The waiter pulled out her chair. Once seated in front of the other place setting at the circular table, Catherine looked from one to the other. "The two of you look like I'm about to impose a life sentence on you."

Luc glanced at Mandy and decided that if they went through with this test, and if he didn't get his testosterone under control, these two weeks would seem like a lifetime.

"Everything's fine," Mandy offered. "We were just speculating on what your plan might entail."

Catherine waved a dismissive hand. "Oh, let's eat first. No sense ruining what could be a perfectly lovely lunch with business talk." Catherine picked up a menu and motioned for the waiter hovering nearby.

Luc drew in a deep breath. He'd been hoping they could get this over with quickly, and then he could make a quiet exit. He should have known it wouldn't be that easy. His life never was.

What seemed like an eternity later, Catherine pushed aside her dessert plate, then sipped her coffee and looked from Luc to Mandy. Setting the cup down, she pointed out the restaurant window to the blue lake.

"That lake and all the land around it once belonged to my grandfather. It's all mine now, but back then, the lake didn't have a name. No one seemed interested in giving it one and just referred to it as *the lake,* so, on my seventeenth birthday I named it Hope."

Wondering if Catherine was making idle conversation, but thinking she'd heard a catch in her voice, Mandy glanced at the older woman. Moisture glistened in her eyes.

She quickly blinked it away and went on. "Everyone thought Lake Hope was just a whimsical title assigned to a nameless landmark by a romantic, fanciful, dreamy-eyed teen. No one but my mother knew that it was for an entirely different reason." Catherine signaled for the waiter to refill her water glass.

Mandy studied her, concerned about the pain in Catherine's voice. When the older woman stared at the filled water glass and didn't make a move to drink, Mandy knew something was wrong.

She touched Catherine's hand where it lay balled in a fist on the tablecloth. "Are you all right?"

As if wakening from a dream, Catherine started slightly, then smiled at Mandy and patted their entwined hands. "Yes, dear, I'm fine."

Mandy glanced at Luc, surprised to see the same concern written across his features and aimed at Catherine. The assessment of hardhearted that she'd assigned to him the evening before shifted just slightly. Maybe a heart did beat under that tailor-made jacket after all.

She shifted her attention back to Catherine, who had taken a drink from her water glass and was just replacing it on the table. The ice cubes tinkling merrily against the glass mocked the suddenly somber mood at the table.

"Perhaps we should discuss the test." Mandy made the suggestion in hope of leading Catherine away from whatever it was that had creased her brow and painted pain in her eyes.

"I'm leading up to that, my dear, if you'll bear with me." Catherine straightened in her chair and cleared her throat. "Often, young girls believe that having a baby is the answer to escaping a family life that is less than happy. Or mistakenly believing that they can hold onto a young man's affections by getting pregnant with his child. What they don't see is the responsibility connected to bringing a life into this world, or that the young man may not want to share in that responsibility. Nor do they see that sometimes, the family may not agree. Since they are underage with no legal rights, they then may have to survive the agony of being separated from that child forever." With pain etched across her elegant face, she looked from Luc to Mandy.

"I don't want either of you to think that my suggestion for this test was made lightly or that I have some sexually perverted streak running through my genes that compels me to arrange illicit affairs. I assure you that my suggestion was made with both an eye for morality and with a great deal of careful thought."

Luc smiled. "I think I can speak for Ms. James and myself when I say that no such thoughts ever crossed our minds, Catherine."

Mandy nodded her agreement. "Absolutely."

"Thank you for assuring me you aren't in doubt as to my sanity or my morals." Catherine smiled, really smiled, for the first time since she'd begun talking about the test. But it was fleeting and replaced seconds later with a serious expression. "That said, I should tell you that I have a vested interest in this little experiment in human nature. The teen that I want to take part in this test is my granddaughter, Shannon."

Luc sucked in a breath.

Mandy reeled from the shock.

Neither of them had to say it, but she was sure that, like her, Luc knew that this raised the stakes more than a few notches.

"Normally, I wouldn't dream of interfering in my children's family matters, but this is an exception. You see" — Catherine took another sip of water — "Shannon is in the throes of her first love. What she doesn't know is that I was there once, and I recognize things in my granddaughter's eyes that I saw in my own. I hear things in her voice. I understand her reasoning, no matter how troublesome it is." She looked from one to the other of her lunch companions. "I'm hoping that her participation in this . . . experiment will make her see that flaw in her thinking."

The hair on Mandy's neck stood on end.

This was the very thing she hoped the introduction of the baby simulators into the school's curriculum would solve. "Has anyone tried to speak to her, make her see reason?"

"Oh my, yes. I have, her mother and father have, and even her clergy. Still she insists that she wants to have a baby. I don't think she understands exactly why she feels the need for a child at fifteen, but I do. She and her parents are not getting along. Her boyfriend is most likely leaving for a West Coast college next year. She's feeling abandoned, unloved. She thinks a baby will not only fill the void, but help her escape her unhappy home life. Little does she know that her parents, my daughter and son-in-law, would never tolerate the stigma *they* feel this would attach to their family."

Glancing first at a thoughtful Luc, Mandy leaned forward. "*They* feel? I take it you don't agree."

"No. That's the kind of reasoning that ruled decades ago. This is a new age, when things like that are no longer frowned upon. However, Shannon is underage, and she has no idea how the child would and could ruin her life. Nor does she understand that, aside from depriving herself of an education and a social life, she would have to endure the agony of having to give the child up." She shook her head. "Her parents are about as straight-laced as they come. They would never insist on abortion, since neither of them believes in it, but they've confided in me that once the baby entered this world, they'd see to it that Shannon never saw the child again."

Luc frowned. Leaning forward and propping his elbows on the table, he centered his gaze on Catherine. "Since the board and you seemed intent on secrecy, with which I totally agree, where then would this *experiment* take place?" He liked *experiment* better than *test*. It made this whole thing seem less like a final exam.

"My lake house," Catherine said without hesitation. Once more, her gaze went to the lake. "Lake Hope is three miles long. At the far end, the least developed because I still own a fair share of it, there is a very comfortable house. I only use it on my birthday. The rest of the year, it stands vacant."

Luc nodded and let his gaze drift to the lake.

Mandy kept her attention on Catherine. "There's more to this than just saving your granddaughter, isn't there?" Out of the corner of her eye, she saw Luc's gaze snap back to them.

The older woman smiled at Mandy. "You are very perceptive, my dear." She sighed. "Yes, there is a great deal more to it."

Intuition told Mandy that what Catherine had withheld was personal. In which case, they had no right prying into it. "If you don't want to share it with us, that's fine. We have all the information we need."

"Not quite. Aside from it ruining her life, I don't want Shannon to have to bear the pain and regret of giving up a child." Catherine hesitated for a few seconds and said, "Hope was my daughter. She was born at the lake house in 1959 on my seventeenth birthday. Back in the fifties, having a child out of wedlock was heavily frowned upon. And the humiliation would have killed my parents." Her voice faltered, and her gaze clouded with memories. "They allowed me to hold her for a few minutes." She flashed her luncheon companions a watery smile. "She was so lovely. So tiny. So. . . ." She took a deep, fortifying breath. "I've searched for her for years, but I never saw her again."

CHAPTER 3

Luc had excused himself from the lunch right after they'd settled on the time and place for the test to begin — Catherine's lake house, next Monday, four days from now. Catherine had assured him she would see to it that he got a two week leave of absence from his job, but that he would be on call for emergencies. Mandy would have to work over the weekend to get everything in her office in order, but if she could accomplish her goal, then it was worth every minute of overtime.

She and Catherine had lingered in the restaurant, sipped coffee, talked about trivial things and avoided the subject Mandy really wanted to discuss, Catherine's daughter. When she decided that Catherine had said all she planned on saying on the subject, Mandy had gone back to work.

Unable to clear her mind of the look of unfathomable pain and loss on Catherine

Daniels' face when she'd talked about Hope, Mandy had driven the long way around the lake. By the time she parked behind the Social Services building, it was well after three, and she still hadn't been able to shake the awful blanket of despondency that Catherine's admission had cast over her.

When Mandy got to her office, she tried to concentrate on the work that needed to be finished before the test began, but found it impossible. All she could think about was the pain in Catherine's eyes and voice when she talked about her daughter. If only she could do something to help her, but she couldn't do it without help, and that would mean divulging Catherine's secret. Maybe she could. . . .

"Ahem."

Mandy roused from her thoughts to find her boss, Rebecca Hart, smiling down at her from the other side of her cluttered desk. She wore her usual casual attire, a pair of faded jeans and a white, Oxford shirt. But her sparkling green eyes and her cheery face, framed by cascading waves of red hair, held warmth and friendliness that drew an observer's gaze and silently told of her warm heart and concern for their clients.

"So, how was lunch with the rich and

famous?"

Mandy played it down. "It was lunch."

"You eat in the most exclusive restaurant in three counties and all you can say is 'it was lunch'?" Becky pushed aside a pile of folders, then sat on the corner of Mandy's desk. "Okay, spill it. Why the frown?"

"Thinking."

"Uh oh," Becky said, shaking her head. "When you think, it always makes work for me. Last time it was finding that Morris girl a home."

Mandy flashed her boss a smile. "You were just as eager to get her out of that house as I was. If we hadn't pulled out all the stops to get her away from that abuse, they'd be fitting her for a body bag. Face it, boss, you're a real softie when it comes to kids."

Picking up Mandy's pen, Becky clicked the point out and began drawing concentric circles on her memo pad. "I know what you're doing, you know?"

Mandy froze. Had her boss heard about the test somehow? "You do?"

"Yup. You're trying to make everyone think I'm a good guy, and it isn't gonna work." She scribbled through the circles. "The word is out that I'm an ogre. Just ask my husband."

Removing her best pen from Becky before she adopted it as she usually did any pen she got her hands on, Mandy grinned. "He's so in love with you, I'm sure he thinks you're flawless." She took a deep breath and voiced the question she knew had to come. "Becky, I'm going to need to take a couple of weeks off." While Becky mulled her request over, Mandy thought about her boss.

No one had to make Becky Hart look good, either morally or physically. She ran a casual office, no suits or pantyhose required. Both she and Mandy usually wore jeans, a nice blouse and sneakers to work. But as casual as she was with her appearance, Becky ran an efficient office. The first one there in the morning and the last to leave at night, she could be called at any time in between to help a child out of a bad home situation or counsel a parent. While she worked tirelessly for the welfare of a child, she also worked to keep the family units in one piece. The difference between her and too many people working in Social Services was that Becky genuinely cared what happened to the people she came in contact with. That her paycheck did not finance Paris vacations didn't enter her mind. Becky was special, somewhat of a rarity when compared to some of the other social workers Mandy had come up against.

"Becky?"

"I'm not sure I can say yes. I have to check the schedule and see what's coming up. Where're you going?"

Mandy shook her head. "Nowhere special, just taking a little R and R at a friend's house out on Lake Hope."

"Well, as long as you aren't leaving town, I'll give you a qualified yes. I still have to check the schedule. Would you be able to come in a day or two if needed?"

Mandy nodded. She'd only be on the other side of the lake. "Sure, and thanks."

Hesitating before she went on, Mandy played with the pen, clicking the point in and out, until it even got on her nerves. Opening her desk drawer, she stuck the pen away, beyond both hers and Becky's reach.

"I appreciate it. . . ." She hated being evasive with her boss. Becky had been very good to her since she'd come to Carson. But the board had made it very clear that this test was to be kept strictly under wraps. No one was to know except the school board, Luc and her. She couldn't risk messing this up because her conscience hurt.

Becky leaned down and looked at Mandy's face half hidden behind a cascade of auburn hair. "Do I hear a but?"

Mandy glanced at her. "There *is* something else."

"I knew it. Let me out of here," Becky said, making as if to sneak out of the office.

It's now or never, Mandy girl. "Do you think you could find someone for me?" she blurted before her nerve could desert her.

Becky's retreat came to a sudden stop. "Depends. Who exactly are you looking for?"

Mandy sat forward, leaning her forearms on the stacks of paper covering her desk top. "This has to be kept totally on the QT. You have to promise not to say a word to anyone, especially anyone in this town. I shudder to think what Laureene Talbot would do with it if she got a hold of it."

"They don't call me lockjaw for nothing." Becky's face transformed into a smile.

Mandy just stared at her. "Promise me, Becky. Please?"

"Okay, okay, I promise." Then the smile vanished, and she leaned her palms on the desk. "But why so serious?"

"Because, if what I'm about to tell you leaks out, this could do irreparable damage to a very prominent citizen of Carson."

"Oh, geeze, Mandy, what have you gotten yourself into now?"

73

Mandy shook her head. "Nothing bad. It's just . . . just . . . just something I *have* to do, but I need your help." She took a deep breath. "I need to find Catherine Daniels' illegitimate daughter."

Becky's jaw dropped. She slowly straightened and chewed on her lower lip, a habit she had adopted when faced with a troublesome dilemma. Mandy's heart plummeted. By her expression, her boss had reservations about helping in the search for Hope.

"Catherine Daniels has an illegitimate child?"

Mandy nodded.

"Of all people, I never would have. . . ." Becky shook her head. "You do realize you're walking into a hornet's nest here?"

Mandy nodded again.

"Did she ask you to do this?"

After a slight hesitation, Mandy murmured, "No."

"Then why are you doing it? I don't like the idea of you butting into Catherine Daniels' private affairs. She could have your job in a blink of an eye. Besides, this girl may not want to be found."

Mandy met Becky's stern expression. "I know that, and if that's the case, we will abide by her wishes and drop the whole thing. Since Catherine has no idea that I'm doing this, and just in case this blows up in my face, and the girl could care less who her real mom is, only you and I will be the wiser. But Catherine told me she's been looking for her for years, so, if we do find Hope, and she is willing to meet with Catherine. . . ." She was babbling to keep Becky from saying no. "If she isn't, we can at least give her the information about her mother, and, if she ever changes her mind, she can come on her own. If we don't find anything at all, then no one will ever know we even tried. But if we do. . . ." Mandy looked Becky dead in the eye. "If we do, Catherine Daniels will be one of the happiest women alive and. . . ." She emphasized the *and*. "If you'd seen the look on her face, the pain when she told me about Hope, you'd know she'll be eternally grateful."

"Eternally grateful, huh?" Becky's brows furrowed in thought.

Mandy knew Becky was mulling over the fundraiser they'd talked about last week to start a shelter for abused women. When her expression showed definite interest, Mandy knew the carrot she'd dangled before the hungry social worker had done its job. She held her breath.

Becky stared at her for a very long moment. "That's a lot of *ifs,* Mandy." She

75

looked to the ceiling as though seeking divine guidance, then back to Mandy. "You're sure Catherine wants to find this girl?"

"Trust me on this, Becky. She's been searching for years. I saw her face when she talked about her. I don't believe there is anything that Catherine Daniels wants more."

Becky blew out a long breath. She propped both hands on her hips, a stance Mandy knew well as her let's-get-this-show-on-the-road posture. Her heart lifted.

"I won't guarantee anything, but. . . ." Then she grinned. "Oh, what the heck, let's go for it."

Luc's day hadn't gone well after he left Catherine and Mandy. He'd just sat down at his desk and started to make a dent in the pile of work awaiting him when the door opened. His secretary barely had time to announce the unscheduled arrival of Mr. and Mrs. Tanner, Jeb Tanner's parents, before they pushed her aside and came rushing into his office.

"Michaels." Jeb's father, the town's mechanic, and his wife brought with them the odor of motor oil. "We need to talk."

Four words that always shot apprehension through Luc when coming from a parent.

Luc extended his hand to the man. "Harry. Linda," he added, nodding at Harry's wife. "Please," he said, gesturing toward the empty chairs facing his desk, "have a seat." Once everyone was settled, he leaned back in his chair. "What can I do for you, Harry?"

"You can stop trying to divert Jeb's attention away from getting that athletic scholarship. He told us what you said about his grades. Right now, with the UCLA scout hot after Carson's star quarterback, Jeb needs to concentrate on his game. The grades can come later."

Luc had to bite his tongue to keep from giving the man a quick lesson on scholastic priorities. When would the people of Carson learn that being able to run a football over a goal line didn't qualify their sons for anything other than a career as a professional athlete. Didn't they realize that with one injury that career could end as quickly as it had begun? That without an education, the benched athlete would have nothing to fall back on?

Harry Tanner leaned forward. "I'll level with you, Michaels. If Jeb doesn't get that scholarship, he can kiss college goodbye. There's no way I can send him on what I make at the garage." He glanced at his wife, then back to Luc. "I don't want my kid working his fingers to the bone in some factory or some . . . garage, then bringing home just enough to make ends meet." His wife took his hand, squeezed it and smiled, as if reassuring him that what he did for a living was good, honest work. "If he gets the scholarship, then he has a chance of getting a decent job."

How many times had Luc heard this same argument? And how did he convince them that Jeb would never get the scholarship unless he maintained a 2.5 GPA, and that he had a better chance at a decent job with high grades than he did with his prowess on the football field?

"Harry, I can see your point. I want what's best for Jeb as much as you do. I also know that Jeb's a bright kid, and I know how good he is on the football field. However, he'll still have to keep his grades up to get the sports scholarship." Luc sighed. "He's going into his senior year, so this is no time to slack off on his studies." He leaned forward, bracing his forearms on the desk. "What if he doesn't get the scholarship?"

Harry Tanner's face paled, and his expression turned to one of sheer panic. "But, Asa said —"

"The final decision rests with UCLA, not Asa Watkins." Luc stood, walked around the desk, and then sat on the corner. "Harry, what I'm trying to tell you is don't let Jeb put all his eggs in one basket. Even if he keeps his grades up, there are no guarantees that he'll get the scholarship. He's just one of hundreds vying for it."

Linda Tanner laid a hand on her husband's arm. "Harry, I think we should listen to Mr. Michaels."

Tanner shook off her hand. "Are you saying my boy's not good enough to win that scholarship?"

Luc shook his head. "Of course not. Jeb's a fine athlete. He's also a good student, when he applies himself. I just think we need to prepare for all eventualities."

Harry Tanner abruptly stood and took his wife's arm, then steered her toward the door. "He'll win it, Michaels. He'll win it if I have to make him practice throwing that ball twenty-four hours a day until next fall when that scout comes back. He *will* win it." He shoved his wife through the door and slammed it hard enough to make the glass in the window behind Luc rattle.

Luc sighed. He hoped for Jeb's sake that his father was right.

When she left work a few days later, Mandy felt quite pleased with herself. She'd worked

79

over the weekend to clear her desk of any pressing business so she could start Catherine's test the next morning. Becky had already initiated the search for Catherine's daughter, and a case Mandy had been working on for weeks had finally seen a happy ending. A foster child had found a permanent home with a family that loved her and wanted her enough to have started adoption proceedings.

Tired, but satisfied, Mandy turned her car down Main Street, heading for the small apartment she'd rented north of town when she had first arrived in Carson. It wasn't much, but she'd decorated it with plants and mementoes that had put her personal stamp on it and quickly transformed the two rooms into a cozy home.

As she drove down the tree-lined streets, she took in the small town that she'd come to love. Stores huddled against each other in a neat row, all painted beige, gray, federal blue, white or tan, colors that the town fathers had designated acceptable. Lining the sidewalks at intervals stood large barrels filled with bright yellow chrysanthemums with green and white vinca cascading over the edges, the fall replacements for the colorful petunias that had grown there all summer. The same fall flowers had been planted in the town square. Dark green and white striped awnings were rolled up to allow the admittance of the late afternoon sun. The few cars, parked diagonally along the curbs, confirmed that most of the town's people were at home enjoying dinner with their families.

Mandy experienced a rush of regret that she wasn't in one of those homes. A flashback intervened of dinner when she'd been growing up. She would have been sitting alone at the table, eating something from a can off a paper plate, while her mother finished the last of her daily bottle of gin.

When the bottle was empty, Connie James would have begun yelling at her small daughter. "If it wasn't for you, I'd have had a good life. Money, friends, a good education, a husband who would care for me, love me and bring home a paycheck."

The words would have been slurred, and soon after, her mother would have fallen into a drunken stupor, leaving Mandy to help her to bed where Connie would remain until the next morning when the whole scenario would begin all over again.

Determinedly, Mandy shook off the memories and concentrated on the beauty of the little town of Carson that surrounded her. About half way down Main Street, she noticed a man walking along the deserted street with his jacket slung over one shoulder.

Even from the back, she recognized him. Luc Michaels. Her heart sped up. Her reaction filled her with apprehension. If simply seeing him walking down the street had that effect on her, what was it going to be like sharing a house with him for two weeks?

As if her heart had turned a deaf ear to her concerns, and before she knew what was happening, she pulled her car to the curb and hit the button to open the automatic window on the passenger's side. The smell of burning leaves and crisp fall air rushed into the car's interior.

"Need a lift?" Was that her voice inviting him into her car? Into these close confines, to sit on the seat next to her, their legs barely inches away? Had she lost her mind?

Luc leaned down and smiled. "I'd love one, thanks." He opened the door and slid in, then slammed it closed and looked at her. "I was thinking the walk home would be refreshing, but I'm afraid my long day is getting to me."

Mandy glanced down at his white shirt front. Moisture had plastered it to his chest. He must not have been wearing anything under it. She could see the swirls of dark chest hair through the material.

Dragging her gaze away, she stared straight ahead, trying to eject the image of Luc without the shirt from her mind and make room for concentration on the road ahead. What had gotten into her? Sex was not something that normally preoccupied her thoughts around men. Why now? And why him of all people?

Whatever the reason, she had to put a stop to it now, while she could. In a few days she'd be living with this man, and lapsing into these sexual fantasies every time they got within sight of each other could get downright dangerous.

Clasping the steering wheel in a death grip, she eased the car away from the curb. "Where's your car?" she asked, pleased to find her vocal chords working better than her common sense.

"The battery went dead. I had to use my lights when I came to work this morning, and since it's an older model without all the fancy bells and whistles to call my attention to it, I guess I forgot to turn them off." While he spoke to her, Luc kept his gaze trained on the passing scenery. "Of course, since I know little or nothing about what goes on under the hood of my car, it could be anything."

"You had to use your lights?" That meant he had come to work before her alarm had even gone off.

He turned to her, his dark brown eyes leaving her breathless. "I wanted to get an early start. There's a lot to be done before we adjourn our lives to Catherine's lake house." He stared at her for a moment and then quickly looked away. "Besides, it's easier to work when there are no kids running in and out, and my secretary isn't routing phone calls through my office."

In complete agreement, Mandy nodded. "I admire anyone who can get up early. I hate mornings." She laughed. "I'm told I'm not the most amiable person until I've had my coffee. Ever see that T-shirt that says *I don't do mornings*?" Luc nodded. "That was designed with me in mind."

She glanced at her passenger. Luc's gaze held hers for only an instant, but it spoke volumes. It told her that he was as aware as she was of the attraction between them.

Rats! How am I going to put up a fight, if he isn't going to resist?

Luc was trying his best to resist the woman behind the wheel, but he seemed to have lost control of his own movements. His mind was flooded with images of Mandy, hair tousled from sleep, her eyes still holding remnants of her dreams, her lips pink and inviting, her —

Wow! He blinked to dispel the images. Then his gaze went to her hands gripping the steering wheel. He studied her long, graceful fingers topped by nails kept serviceably short and coated with clear nail polish. He imagined those nails digging into his flesh in the throes of passion.

Tearing his gaze from her hands, he let it settle on the auburn hair falling over her bare shoulders in soft waves. Again his imagination betrayed him and gave him a sampling of how those tresses would feel falling over his body.

Once more, he snatched his gaze away, searching for somewhere safe to allow it to settle. As if magnetized, it went to her long, tanned legs. Before his imagination could kick in again, he sighed and closed his eyes.

"Are you going to sleep, or are you going to tell me where you live?"

Without opening his eyes, Luc replied, "27 North Elm Street." He cracked his eyes open a sliver. "Turn right at the next stop sign, then left."

Moments later, the car glided to a stop. He opened his eyes.

"Home sweet home," Mandy said.

Was she being sarcastic? He glanced at her and found her staring raptly at the house. Her gaze echoed his own feelings every time he came home.

The white, Cape Cod structure brought a rush of warmth and security to him. Aside from his job, this house was the most important thing in Luc's life. To Luc, everything about it, the variegated chrysanthemums he'd planted last week beneath the boxwood hedges, the white picket fence, the verdant lawn, even the swing on the front porch, symbolized a stable existence. Most of all it was home — a real home, the place one returned to day after day, year after year.

Nothing is forever, came his father's reminder.

"It's . . . lovely," she whispered, interrupting his thoughts. "So welcoming and homey." She shifted her gaze to him. "You must love it here."

"Very much."

Her gaze went back to the house and filled with a sad longing. He knew that look and the desperate loneliness it embodied. "It's the only real home I've ever known." Now, why had he told her that?

"Really?" Then she dipped her head, hiding the pink he'd noted rising in her cheeks behind the cascade of her hair. "That's right. You said you were raised in military schools." She raised her head, then tossed her long hair over her shoulder and looked him in the eye. "I am truly sorry about the abstinence crack the other night."

Knowing that truce between them would make the next two weeks easier all around, he smiled. "Apology accepted. I'm afraid I should also apologize. I baited you and deserved your anger."

Her brow furrowed. "Baited me? How?"

"I thought that if I could make you uneasy, you might slip up and blow your presentation." He gazed out the windshield, thinking about how in control she'd been, except for that one mistake. "Actually, I was very impressed with your thorough knowledge of your subject matter. You had all your bases more than covered."

"I know you don't approve of it, but this project means a lot to me."

He recalled thinking at the meeting that that there was more to this project than just saving the town's teens from unwanted pregnancy. The same feeling washed over him now. He turned to face her. "Why?"

"Why?"

"Why is this project so important to you? It's commendable that you want to help the kids in Carson, but there's more to it than that, isn't there?"

She looked away, but not before he saw the flash of pain across her features. Had she been one of the pregnant teen statistics? He glanced at her trim figure. She didn't have the fullness that a woman retained after carrying a child. Having been blamed repeatedly for his mother's less than sultry figure, he knew all about the effects of pregnancy on a woman's body. So, why then was Mandy James so devoted to this?

"It's a very long story, and I'm sure you're as anxious to relax and get out of your work clothes as I am. Maybe I'll tell you some other time."

Luc didn't push. He had a whole two weeks to get Mandy to talk about herself. One hand on the door handle, the other clutching his jacket and briefcase, Luc turned to her. "Thanks . . . for the ride and the apology."

"No problem."

She smiled, and his heart skipped a beat. Before he could stop himself or think about the consequences, he leaned forward, his gaze centered on her delectable lips. He blinked, cleared his throat, and then quickly pulled back. Without another word or glance at Mandy, he exited the car.

Mandy sat in her car, in front of Luc Michaels' house for a full five minutes before she could think coherently enough to drive away.

Tentatively, she touched her mouth with her fingertips. Her other hand lay over her chest, trying to still her pounding heart. She couldn't believe what had just happened. She'd just sat here like a big dummy and nearly let Lucas Michaels kiss her.

Was she nuts?

Have you lost what's left of your mind?

Luc leaned against the inside of his front door. Sweat beaded his brow. He'd actually been going to kiss her. Worse yet, if he'd read her right, she would have let him.

He dropped his briefcase and suit jacket on the hall table and headed into the living room to the small corner bar. Without hesitation, he poured himself two fingers of good Scotch and drank it down in one gulp. Coughing at the burning sensation that seared his throat membranes, he sat the empty glass down and threw himself on the sofa.

He'd barely had time to start gathering his thoughts when the phone rang. Sighing, he picked up the receiver.

"Hello."

"Michaels? Harry Tanner. I just picked up your car. Before I start anything, I wanted to let you know that it's not just a dead battery like you thought." Tanner's curt voice betrayed that he was still upset with his son's principal.

Luc leaned his head back against the sofa and closed his eyes in preparation for the bad news. "What is it?"

"It's your alternator. Seeing as how this is an older model, I don't have one in stock. I'll have to send to Charleston for a new one."

Luc wondered if this was punishment for butting into Tanner's son's business, or if the problem was legitimate. Either way, he had no choice. Tanner was the only garage mechanic in town.

"How long will it take to fix it?"

"Well . . . with the time to get the part over here, I'd say you better plan on being without a car for at least four or five days."

Great. Just long enough for him to have to beg a ride out to Catherine's lake house to begin the test. And, since Catherine would be picking up her granddaughter, and no one else knew about this test run except the board of education, which he was not ready to interact with on any level yet, that meant begging a ride from Mandy. He rubbed his hands over his eyes.

"Take as long as you need," he finally said, then hung up the phone.

He picked up the remote and clicked on the TV, hoping to catch the last of the first game of the World Series. But even as the TV screen came alive with the game, his concentration wasn't on baseball. Instead, an image of Mandy walking across the restaurant dining room flooded his mind.

Luc sighed and leaned his head against the sofa back. Maybe, between now and then, he'd be able to get his libido under control.

Maybe.

CHAPTER 4

The following morning, when the phone rang, Mandy had just zipped up her suitcase and dragged it into the living room and set it beside another one of equal size. On top of the larger one sat the box that held the baby simulator.

Impatient at the delay, she grabbed the receiver and barked into the phone. "Hello."

A pause, then, "Mandy, it's Luc. My car's not going to be ready for a few days. Would it be too much trouble for you to swing by my house and pick me up on your way to the lake house?"

Her heart skipped a beat. Did she want to say yes and be trapped in the close confines of a car with him again? She hesitated, then took a deep breath and mentally shrugged. In a couple of hours she would be with Luc for fourteen days, so what harm could a bit more time do at this point? "Sure. No trouble at all. I was just getting ready to leave. I can be there in about twenty minutes."

"Thanks. See you in a few." The phone went dead.

Twenty minutes later Mandy parked in front of Luc's house. He was waiting on the front porch with a medium size suitcase beside him and a travel mug in his hand. She watched him hurry down the path to her car and wondered how men seemed able to survive with fewer clothes than women for the same period of time.

She pushed a button on the dash to pop the trunk and waited while he threw his luggage in beside hers. Then he climbed into the passenger seat. The aroma of his aftershave wafted to her on the breeze the open door admitted. She took a deep breath, then immediately realized that hadn't been one of her smarter moves. She quickly hit the button to roll down her window.

He settled into the seat and turned to her. "I appreciate this. It seems that one of the drawbacks of owning an older car is that replacement parts have to be ordered."

Mandy frowned. "I thought you said it was just a dead battery."

He laughed. "I also said I had little to no knowledge of what goes on under my car's hood. I was wrong about the battery. Seems the alternator quit and has to be special ordered. I should have wheels again in a few days."

Mandy nodded as if she knew what an alternator was and pulled away from the curb. As they headed toward Lake Hope, the silence in the car grew deafening. "So, are you ready for our grand adventure?"

Luc shifted his position in the seat. "Not really."

"Oh?"

"Well, I've never been a father, and I didn't have the greatest role model to call on for points of reference." He realized he'd just opened the door to a subject he'd rather not get into. To prevent questions, he turned the conversation on her. "What about you?"

For a long time she remained fixated on the road. She and Luc had been cast in the role of parents to a teenage mother, Catherine's granddaughter, and a mechanical baby, and Mandy suddenly realized she was no better equipped for it than Luc. "Like you, I've never played this part before, and I don't have any reference points either." She glanced at him, then back to the road. "Guess we'll have to play it by ear."

The conversation came to an abrupt halt. Neither of them, it seemed, was willing to

94

elaborate.

When Mandy had driven around the lake after having lunch with Catherine and Luc, she hadn't been able to see Catherine's summer house for the thick stand of trees blocking her view. So, as she pulled into the driveway that wound around to the front of the house, her breath caught in her throat. Without even glimpsing the inside, she felt certain that the entire pitiful shack she'd grown up in would easily fit into just one of the rooms.

Having come from the small coal town with the contradictory name of Pleas-antville, a lot smaller and much poorer than Carson, she'd never seen anything this imposing or this elegant. She supposed her hometown had once been a *pleasant* village, until the mine closed, leaving those who hadn't fled to live in rundown houses that screamed of the poverty inside.

Catherine Daniels' towering two-story, stone house nestled in the grove of white oaks and maple trees like a behemoth hiding from the world. Looking more like a castle with a turret on one side and an octagonal set of upper story bay windows on the other, it spoke of old world charm and elegance. A wrap-around porch dotted with white wicker rockers and supported by white columns with stone bases, gave anyone who wished to sit there a panoramic view of Lake Hope. Mandy wondered absently how many hours Catherine must have sat there thinking about the daughter she'd lost.

The lawn, arrayed with brilliant fall flower gardens, was dotted with the first colorful fallen leaves of the season and stretched to the lake's edge where a pier protruded out into the water like a long boney finger.

Mandy sighed with pleasure. Spending time here, no matter how brief, was definitely not going to be a hardship.

"Impressive." Luc's voice pulled Mandy from her perusal of what would be their home for the next fourteen days.

"To say the least," she muttered, still gazing wide-eyed at the house.

Just then, the front door opened, and Catherine Daniels stepped out on the porch and beckoned for them to join her. Beside her stood a jeans and T-shirt clad young girl with an excited, expectant smile curving her lips and ash blond hair pulled back in a ponytail that reached well past her shoulders.

Mandy stepped through the large, oak doors

into a foyer that stopped her cold in her tracks. The only thing more breathtaking than the outside of the house was the inside. From where she stood, she could see two huge rooms, both filled with what looked like antique furniture and chandeliers hanging from the high ceilings and dripping with diamond-cut crystals

"Let's go into the family room, and I'll make the introductions there." Catherine led the group down a long hall toward the back of the sprawling house.

Mandy couldn't believe this was a summer house and had to wonder what Catherine's year-round residence looked like. While Mandy continued to take in her surroundings, she, Luc and the young girl followed Catherine down the hall.

When they arrived at the family room, Mandy was again taken aback. While the rest of the rooms boasted antique, Victorian style furniture, this room looked as if it had fallen from the pages of this month's *Better Homes and Gardens.* While large, the room was furnished in a very laid-back style with a huge fieldstone fireplace as its focal point. Beside the fireplace, recessed in a bookcase holding books and what appeared to be a combination DVD and satellite TV box, was a jumbo, flat-screen TV. Surrounding the fireplace, a grouping of occasional tables, overstuffed sofas and chairs formed a cozy conversation area and provided the perfect place for a family to gather in informal comfort at the end of a day. In a far corner, in front of a wall of French doors, a pool table took up most of that end of the floor.

Catherine motioned them to the sitting area. "I had this room redecorated strictly with creature comfort and family in mind," she said, taking a seat in a large chair with a footstool. "I never liked the straight back Victorian sofas and chairs my mother favored."

Mandy and Luc took seats on the sofa facing Catherine, and the young girl plopped cross-legged on the ottoman at her grandmother's feet.

"This young lady," Catherine motioned to the girl, "is my granddaughter, Shannon Cameron. Shannon lives in Carson, but attends a private school in Charleston. She'll be the teenager taking part in this experiment. Her mother and father have given their written consent." She removed a sheet of paper from the table to her right and handed it to Mandy. "Shannon, this is Lucas Michaels and Amantha James. I'm sure they won't object to you calling them Luc and Mandy." She looked to Mandy for affirmation. Receiving a nod, Catherine went on. "While they're here with you, you will afford them the same respect you would your parents."

The girl nodded, lowered her feet to the floor and leaned toward Mandy. "May I see the baby now?"

"It's in the car —"

"I'll get it." Luc jumped to his feet. Before Mandy could reply, he was out of the room. Moments later, they heard the front door close.

While Shannon glanced expectantly at the door, and they waited for Luc to come back, Catherine told Mandy that she had filled the pantry and fridge with provisions and had the electric, water and phone turned on. All the time, Shannon, who appeared to be ready to jump out of her skin, continued to monitor the empty doorway. Mandy could tell by the excited expression on the girl's face that she was really looking forward to getting started. Having seen the effect of the baby simulator on young girls initially, and then after a few days of baby-care confinement, she felt certain that the excitement would soon wane.

If all went as she expected, the school board and Lucas Michaels were in for a big eye-opener.

■ ■ ■ ■

Thankful to be out of that room, Luc stepped onto the wide porch and drew in a long breath of the lake air. Slowly, the tightness that had gathered in his chest eased away.

Sitting there with those three women had brought back stifling memories of scenes from his childhood. His mother's twice-weekly "teas" were nothing more than her way of holding court and lording it over the wives of officers who served under Luc's father.

It had been bad enough that she'd insisted five-year-old Luc be present, washed, combed and wearing his Sunday best. Added to that was her insistence that he sit quietly, hands folded in his lap for what seemed to him like days, while she alternately fussed over him like some well-deserved trophy and soaked up the phony compliments from her so-called friends, and then totally ignored him.

Sometimes the officers' wives brought their kids, and Luc was excused to play with them. But he was careful not to make friends, because he'd learned at an earlier age that — as his father always told him —

nothing is forever, and if he didn't get too fond of anyone, then it hurt less when they had to move again.

Shaking off the memories, Luc went to get the box containing *robo* baby from the car. Seeing the luggage, he decided to bring that in as well to afford himself a little extra time to pull himself together.

Sufficiently back in control of himself, Luc returned to the Daniels' family room almost fifteen minutes later carrying a long box. The room went silent. All eyes locked on the box. It seemed to double in weight. He shifted it slightly, wondering if it held the end of his life in Carson.

"I brought in the luggage, too. It's in the hall." He handed the box to Mandy.

Shannon jumped to her feet, nearly knocking Luc over in her haste, and came to stand beside Mandy. Mandy placed the box on the floor at her feet and then opened the flaps to reveal an anatomically correct, very real looking, naked baby boy.

"It's a boy, Gram!" Shannon reached into the box, carefully lifted the baby, and cradled it lovingly in her arms. "I was so hoping it would be a boy. I'm gonna name him Joey. Isn't he adorable?" She carried the baby to her grandmother and leaned down to show her.

"Yes, dear, adorable." Catherine smiled at her granddaughter, but Luc could read the apprehension in the woman's face.

Luc chanced a glance at Mandy, doing nothing to suppress the broad, self-satisfied smile on his face. His blatant confidence was met with a silent challenge from Mandy, which he had no trouble reading.

Enjoy it now, Luc. Things will change.

We'll see, he mouthed, still smiling.

She smiled back at him. His pulse rate jumped a notch. For a moment, he couldn't focus on anything around him. He took a deep breath and quickly dragged his gaze from her and centered it on the young girl.

"I'm going to go dress him in the clothes I brought with me." Shannon turned to leave.

Mandy stopped her. "Before you can interact with him, I have to explain to you how this works."

Shannon retook her seat on the ottoman and held Joey in the crook of her arm, casting loving glances at him from time to time. Mandy extracted a small laptop from the box and what looked like a hospital bracelet with a small key attached.

"I need to put this on you." Shannon held out her arm, and Mandy attached the bracelet to the girl's wrist. "I've prepro-

102

grammed the baby, the laptop and the bracelet to interact. It will transmit to the laptop what kind of care you give Joey by picking up the wireless signal from the monitor in the baby's back and recording it. Only you can tend to him. That means if he wakes up in the middle of the night, you must get up and do whatever is necessary to stop his crying. Understand?"

Shannon nodded.

"The key can be inserted in his back to stop the crying, but will not necessarily stop it immediately or without the care he's in need of. It's up to you to figure out what he needs just as any mother would have to do with an infant."

Shannon stood. "Is that all? May I go dress him now?"

Luc wasn't sure Shannon had absorbed anything Mandy had said, but she smiled. "Yes, that's all. If you have any questions, let me know."

Shannon hurried from the room, Joey still cradled in her arms. The tattoo of her footsteps on the stairs echoed down the hall and into the family room.

Catherine stood and walked to the fireplace, then turned toward them, her expression clearly troubled. "She looks terribly excited about all this."

"She certainly does," Luc added. He'd come into this with serious reservations about his success, but Shannon's reaction to the baby had given him the boost of confidence he needed. "Don't you agree?" he asked Mandy.

Mandy ignored him. "It's the first day. She'll soon find out that having an infant around isn't like playing dolls. As the labor-intense days and sleepless nights wear on, the enthusiasm should wane."

"You hope." Luc kept his gloating voice quiet enough so it wouldn't carry to Catherine, but loud enough so Mandy would hear him.

Mandy glared at him. The sanctimonious jerk thought he'd already won the war, but this was one small battle. However, though outwardly calm, she had to admit that Shannon's unprecedented enthusiasm had put a tiny crack in her certainty of success.

And, despite Luc's pronouncement that Mandy was *hoping* for success, she knew that, for her, *hope* didn't play into this. Complete success was an absolute must, and nothing less would do.

CHAPTER 5

Mandy pulled a carton of eggs from the refrigerator and placed them on the counter beside the rest of the breakfast makings. She'd set the table in the bay window overlooking the deck for three and poured each of them a glass of orange juice. As soon as Luc and Shannon came down, she would begin cooking. . . . Correction, *they* would begin cooking.

Last evening, Shannon had taken a sandwich to her room so she could spend time with Joey. Luc had loaded a tray with his supper and carried it into the family room to catch the Yankee game on TV. That left Mandy in the kitchen eating alone and trying to quell her anger at their desertion by reading a book. She'd made up her mind that would not happen again. If this situation was to emulate family life, then they needed to start acting like one.

She'd already announced to both Luc and

Shannon as they'd headed off to bed the previous evening that they would be eating breakfast like a normal family . . . together . . . at the kitchen table. If this experiment was to work, they had to show Shannon how taking care of an infant could interfere with her life — both social and family.

While she waited for Luc and Shannon, she poured herself a cup of coffee and wandered out on the deck. The invigorating, crisp morning air held a distinct hint of the cold weather to come. She shivered and stepped into a puddle of sunlight. Fall was definitely in the air. But she knew that in a few weeks they'd have a spate of warm weather.

She sipped her coffee, and visions of her childhood and running through the fields on a warm Indian Summer day raced through her mind. Without warning, those pleasant memories were shoved aside by recollections of the mornings when her mother was too hung over to make breakfast for her little girl before she went to school. At the age of seven, Mandy would wrestle a carton of milk from the fridge and pour it over a bowl of cold cereal only to find the milk had soured. She soon learned that saying anything to her mother only brought on one of her endless tirades about how much better her life would have been if she hadn't been saddled with a kid she never wanted.

On more mornings than Mandy could count she'd gone to school without anything to eat. Perhaps that's why breakfast was now her favorite meal of the day.

The door to the deck opened, and she turned to find Luc standing behind her, a mug of steaming coffee clutched in his hand. His hair was still damp from his shower, and he wore snug jeans and a lemon yellow, long-sleeved shirt that accentuated the muscles hidden beneath the fabric. Before she could get a handle on her emotions, her heartbeat sped up, and her hands shook, despite being wrapped around a hot coffee cup.

"Morning," he drawled. His sleepy, smoky voice brought a new shiver coursing over her, but definitely not from the chilly weather.

Keeping his gaze on the expanse of blue water beyond the shore, he took a few steps forward, bringing him beside her and way too close for comfort. She felt the heat emanating from his body.

Startled by and unprepared for his sudden and unexpected appearance and her reaction, she swallowed repeatedly to dislodge the thick knot of crazy emotions that had settled in her throat. That being unsuccessful, she took a swig of her coffee and cleared her throat.

"Morning." She moved casually away and leaned on the railing, also training her gaze on the lake.

"Beautiful," he murmured.

"Yes, it is."

"I didn't mean the lake."

Mandy's head snapped around to face him. He was staring at her, his dark eyes warm and . . . inviting. Then he blinked and turned away, and she had to wonder if she'd seen anything there at all.

"I was referring to the changing color of the trees," he said quickly. "In a few weeks they'll be breathtaking."

Luc could have bitten off his own tongue. The words had passed his lips before his brain went into gear. He could blame it on not being fully awake yet, but that would be a lie. With the breeze ruffling her hair, and her face washed in morning sunlight, Mandy was beautiful, no question about it. But he had never intended to voice his thoughts out loud.

"I thought we were having breakfast." A sleepy Shannon clad in pink pajamas stood in the doorway rubbing her eyes.

"We are," Mandy abruptly announced and hurried into the house.

Luc followed, trying not to look at the way her hips swayed or how her hair caressed her shoulders as she walked. Man, he had to get a grip. They still had twelve days to go. How would he manage it if he kept this up? Yes, Mandy was drop-dead gorgeous. Yes, she brought his libido to life like few other women had in recent memory . . . maybe never. Yes, she represented a temptation that went beyond anything he'd come up against before. That didn't mean he had to give in to the fantasies running through his head. He had a way of life he treasured to protect. And he couldn't do that if he didn't stay clear-minded and focused.

Luc took a seat at the table and picked up the newspaper lying folded beside his orange juice glass. He set his coffee cup aside and opened the paper to the sports section. He'd just started reading when the paper flew from his grasp.

"Breakfast is a family project. That means we all pitch in. You can cook this," Mandy announced, laying the newspaper on the counter and then handing him the bacon and a fork. "You do know how to cook bacon, right?"

"Have you forgotten that I live alone?" he

countered, taking the package from her. "If I don't cook, I don't eat." He rose and went to the stove.

"You can toast these." Mandy handed Shannon the package of English muffins.

Shannon dragged her body from the chair and ambled to the toaster. She mumbled something incoherent and slid a muffin from the package. When she tried to stuff the uncut muffin into the toaster slot, Mandy stopped her.

"You have to split them in two. Haven't you ever done this before?"

"No. The cook makes breakfast at our house."

Luc's heart dropped. If she couldn't toast a muffin, how was she going to care for the *robo* baby?

"Well, for the next twelve days, *we* do the cooking, so get used to it." Mandy showed Shannon how to use the fork to break the muffin into two halves and handed them back to her.

When breakfast was cooked and on the table, they all took their seats. Halfway through the meal, a high-pitched cry came from upstairs. Shannon glanced at her unfinished breakfast, then at Mandy.

Luc waited.

Mandy continued eating.

Shannon jumped up from the table. "Don't throw that out. I'll be back after I see to Joey," she called over her shoulder.

She headed toward the back stairs, and to Luc's surprise, she didn't seem at all upset about leaving a hot breakfast behind. He glanced at Mandy, who had a serious, thoughtful expression on her face as she watched Shannon climb the stairs.

"Worried?"

Mandy started. "What? Oh, no, I'm not worried."

He didn't believe her.

"I have to go into town to drop off some paperwork at my office. Do you want me to pick anything up for you?"

Hmm. Changing the subject. She was worried.

He shook his head. "Nothing I can think of, thanks."

A short time later, after they'd finished eating, Mandy began cleaning away the dishes. Luc grabbed the butter and put it in the fridge.

Just then, the phone rang. Luc, being closer, grabbed it. "Hello."

"May I speak to Luc Michaels?" an unfamiliar voice asked.

"This is Luc Michaels."

"This is Tom Fenway at Tanner's Garage.

111

Mr. Tanner asked me to let you know the part for your car came in early, and it's ready for you to pick up anytime now."

"Thanks. I'll be there as soon as I can." He hung up and turned to Mandy. "Can I hitch a ride into town with you? My car's ready earlier than expected."

Mandy had hoped to escape Luc's mesmerizing presence for a few hours, but it looked like she could hang up that hope. However, a sudden idea came to her. "Sure. Let me finish cleaning up here, and I'll be ready to leave. Can you tell Shannon?"

"Tell me what?"

They both turned to find Shannon, who stood just inside the door fully dressed and holding a pajama-clad Joey.

"We have to go to town for a few hours," Mandy explained.

"Can I go with you? It won't take a second to get Joey ready to leave." The eagerness in the girl's voice was more than evident.

"Sure," Luc said.

"That's not possible," Mandy said, feeling like the big rain cloud that had washed out the church picnic.

"Why?"

To her surprise, it was Luc who asked the question and not Shannon. "We don't have a car seat for him. Without it, we'd be putting Joey's safety at risk, and Shannon will earn demerits."

The eagerness vanished from Shannon's face. The crushed expression that replaced it signaled the first signs of regret that she was saddled with Joey's care.

"Can't we just strap him in with a seatbelt? Or Shannon could hold him on her lap and put the belt around both of them."

Mandy shook her head. "State law says he must have a car seat."

She didn't miss the sympathetic look Luc cast at Shannon.

As they pulled out of the driveway, Luc settled back in the seat. "Was that necessary?"

Mandy glanced at him. "What?"

"Not allowing her to come with us just because there's no seat for the *robo* baby?"

Slightly miffed that he still referred to Joey as *the robo baby,* Mandy tightened her hands on the steering wheel and held back her retort. "If we don't think of Joey as a real child, Shannon won't be getting the benefits of the full experience of being responsible for an infant."

Luc raised an eyebrow. "Are you sure you're not sabotaging this whole thing in your favor?"

Mandy pulled to the side of the road and slammed on the brakes. She turned on him like an angry dog. "I resent your insinuation that I would do anything to swing this in my favor. I'm doing everything I can to be fair. That doesn't mean that I'll cut corners for Shannon to make this easier. That would defeat the whole purpose of this test. She has to understand that having a newborn baby to care for is going to put limitations on her life, both physically and socially. Otherwise, there's no point in even continuing with the test." She turned away, slammed the car into drive and pulled back on the road. "And I would appreciate it if you stopped calling Joey *robo baby,* especially in front of Shannon."

After Mandy's tirade, checking his torso for blood entered Luc's mind. For a little thing she sure had a temper. He made a mental note to be more circumspect in the way that he teased her from now on.

For the remainder of the ride, he refrained from talking to Mandy, who suddenly seemed bent on getting to town as quickly as possible. As the car jostled and bumped over potholes, Luc occupied himself with looking at the scenery that whizzed past the passenger side window. As they neared the outskirts of Carson, Mandy slowed down.

Evidently their NASCAR racing speed to get here had burned out her anger.

Instead of heading for Main Street, where Tanner's Garage was located, she turned onto a side street. They crossed a set of railroad tracks, and as they drove on, the neighborhood deteriorated rapidly. Gone were the neat houses with flowers blooming around their foundations. Green lawns were replaced by bare earth cluttered with discarded cars and other junk. Fences lay broken, and gates hung on one hinge, if they hung at all. Broken windows in the houses had been covered with pieces of cardboard or stuffed with dirty rags. Poverty obviously reigned supreme here.

Luc had only been in this part of town a few times before. It was no less depressing than it had been on his previous visits to roust out hooky playing teens. "Where're we going?"

"I have a stop to make before I go to the office." Mandy glanced at him, then back to the road. "I have to check on one of my clients."

A few minutes later she stopped in front of a rundown house that Luc suspected was once someone's garage and had been converted into a very small house. However, this house stood out from the rest. The occupants had obviously made an effort to clean it up. The structure was sorely in need of paint, but no junk littered the grass-spotted yard, and all the windows were intact. A pathetic pot of bright yellow chrysanthemums sat on the front porch.

Mandy shut off the car's engine and turned to Luc. "Come in with me."

His first impulse was to decline, but then he wondered if perhaps there was an irate husband or father in there that posed a threat to Mandy. Although, after the way she'd dressed him down, he didn't see her as needing protection from anyone, the idea that someone might hurt her caused him deep concern and gave him the push he needed to accompany her.

"Let's go." He climbed from the car, totally unprepared for whatever lay behind the unpainted door.

CHAPTER 6

Luc followed Mandy to the front door of the little rundown house. No sooner had she knocked than a high-pitched wail that reminded him of the *robo* baby emanated from inside.

"Who is it?" The answering voice sounded like that of a young girl.

"It's Mandy, Alyce."

"Come on in," the girl called back.

Luc waited while Mandy opened the door and motioned him to accompany her inside. The little house, while definitely in need of work, was dust free and swept clean, but cluttered. Baby clothes in need of folding were piled on a threadbare chair. A pair of running shoes was tucked under the scarred coffee table, and several dirty dishes and an empty baby bottle sat on top. An open book lay face down on the sofa.

Just then a harried looking, young girl, who couldn't have been more than seventeen, emerged from a side room carrying a crying infant of perhaps six months. The girl was dressed in what Luc recognized as the uniform of one of Terri's Tearoom waitresses. Her hair needed combing, and her face was devoid of makeup. The purplish circles beneath her eyes attested to a lack of sleep.

"Lucas Michaels, this is Alyce Walker."

"Hello, Alyce."

"Hey." The baby's crying had subsided to a few hiccups. "I didn't expect you until Wednesday, Ms. James." Alyce shifted the baby to her shoulder and gently rubbed its back.

"I was in the neighborhood and thought I'd stop by to see how things are going." Mandy didn't look at Luc. Probably because he knew she was lying about being in the neighborhood. "How's Lili doing?"

Alyce looked down at the baby. "She had a bad night last night. Neither of us got to sleep until after four. I think she had a tummy ache." Alyce collapsed on the sofa. "I'm working a double shift today, and I'm beat already. I'll be half dead when I come home."

Mandy sat down next to her and took the baby. "Have you done anything about signing up for your GED?" She began to gently

118

rock the baby, and soon its eyes closed in sleep.

Alyce sighed and leaned back against the sofa. "I haven't had time. It seems every time I get a spare minute, Lili needs something. Between her and work, my day is shot."

Luc had been listening silently to the conversation, but this was something he could take care of. "Alyce, I'm the high school principal. If you get your information to me, I can arrange for you to take the courses, if you'd like. I can get the papers you'll need to fill out and give them to Mandy for you. Then it'll just be a case of you taking the classes and passing the final exam."

Alyce's face lit up for a moment, and then the excitement died like an extinguished candle. "I don't know when I'd have time to take the classes. Lili takes up so much of my time, and then there's the babysitter problem. I can't afford to pay anyone to watch her."

"No need to give that a thought." The voice that came from the door Luc had neglected to close behind him startled them all. Granny Jo Hawks stood in the doorway. She stepped into the house and scooped Lili from Mandy's arms. Lili woke up and emitted a faint cry. "I can watch this precious little one while you get your diploma. Got nothing else to do."

"But I can't pay —"

"Did I say anything about wanting to get paid?" Granny smiled. "I have no need for extra money." She winked at Luc. "I'd probably just squander it on nonsense anyway."

Mandy stood. "Then it's settled. Luc will arrange for the classes and testing, and Granny will watch Lili."

A lone tear slid down Alyce's cheek. "I don't know what to say."

Luc smiled. "Just say you'll do it. You have no excuse not to now."

Alyce looked from one to the other of them. Finally, she nodded. "Okay. I'll do it."

"That's my girl. Now you go finish getting yourself dressed for work, and Lili and I will settle in for a girl's night." Granny Jo flashed a beaming smile.

Alyce grinned, then jumped to her feet, hurried into a room off the living area and closed the door. Granny lowered herself into a rocker and began rocking the baby. Moments later, Lili's eyes drifted shut.

Luc smiled at Granny Jo, amazed at how quickly she'd been able to put the child back to sleep. "I take it that you're babysitting?"

"Yep. I take care of Lili a couple times a week so Alyce can go to work. Been doing it almost since this sweet little girl came into this world. That girl's a good momma and proud as they come, but she can't do it all by herself." She shook her head and made a *tsking* sound with her tongue. "Her own family disowned her when Alyce got in the family way. Won't have anything to do with her. Her momma said her life had been ruined by Alyce, and she wasn't gonna let Alyce's brat ruin it further. So, somebody had to step in and help out."

Luc noticed that Mandy flinched when Granny talked about Alyce's mother and how she thought Alyce had ruined her life. Was that just sympathy for Alyce, or had it touched a raw spot in Mandy? Having seen her passion for this project and the way she fought for it at the school board meeting, he'd come to believe she was driven by more than just her job or a social obligation to these teens.

On the ride to the garage to pick up his car, Luc was silent. His thoughts, however, were not. He couldn't get Alyce and Lili and their lot in life out of his mind.

His father's philosophy that *nothing is forever* had been ingrained in Luc and, over the years, had colored much of his thinking, but after witnessing the kind of life Alyce led, he wondered if that prediction applied to this young girl. With a baby to support, no education and a dead-end job waiting tables, he didn't see how she could do it, even with a GED. Where would she find the time and money to pursue a career that would provide a good enough living to leave her present lifestyle behind? All in all, this looked a lot like *forever* to him.

He couldn't imagine Shannon's family allowing her to live under these conditions, but he had to wonder how many other teen moms, who didn't come from affluence, or whose families had disowned them or didn't have benevolent neighbors like Granny Jo, had to endure these hardships alone. And what about the children? Did they, like Alyce's mother, live with resentment because their teen years had been stolen from them by an unwanted, unplanned for child?

Suddenly, the guilt he'd been feeling about going along with Asa's plan to keep the *robo* babies out of the Family Planning classes felt like he had the *Queen Mary*'s anchor on his shoulders.

But he also kept coming back to Mandy's

reaction to Granny's statement about Alyce's mother. At first, he'd thought he'd imagined her reaction, but the more thought he gave it, the more he was convinced it had struck a raw nerve. Was that why this project had become an obsession with her? Had she lived that life?

When Luc arrived back at the lake house, he looked surprised to find Mandy on the porch reading a book. At breakfast she'd told him she'd had work to catch up on at her office. He got out of the car, strolled to porch and flopped down in the rocker beside her.

"I thought you were going to work at your office."

She glanced up from her book. "I was, but I decided that I'd like to come back here and just soak up the peace and quiet. Going to see Alyce always —" She couldn't finish. "I just hope Lili has a better life than most of those babies born to mothers too young to take care of them and love them, or who feel they've ruined their lives just by being born."

"Alyce seems to adore Lili, so I don't think that will be the case." He was silent for a few moments. "What about the father?"

Mandy shook her head. "He decided his life without encumbrances was more important and signed over all rights to the child."

"Doesn't he pay support?"

Again, Mandy shook her head. "Alyce said if he disowned their child, then she didn't want anything from him but his absence. In this instance, instead of the mother feeling like the child ruined her life, the father was afraid Lili would ruin his."

Mandy could feel him staring at her. She glanced nervously out over the smooth lake. Not a ripple shown in its glassy surface. When she realized he was still staring at her, she dipped her head as if going back to her reading. But reading was far from her mind. Visiting Alyce today had brought a lot of memories to the surface that she'd spent years keeping hidden.

She wondered if Alyce would one day look at Lili and accuse her of ruining her life. That precious little bundle had no idea what her life could become and how worthless her mother's cutting remarks could make her feel.

"You're one of them, aren't you?"

"No." Had her answer been too sharp? Had that coupled with her statement about kids ruining lives given too much away? She tried to cover it up with an innocent question, but in her gut she knew it was too late. "One of who?"

"Those unwanted babies. That's why you work so hard at making their lives tolerable and preventing what Alyce is enduring from happening to other young girls."

She sprang out of the rocker and started toward the front door. No one knew about her childhood, and she planned on keeping it that way. The humiliation of having people feel sorry for her because her mother neither loved nor wanted her was something she hated. She'd had enough of that in school and didn't discuss it with anyone, and she was not about to discuss it with Lucas Michaels.

He stopped her with a gentle hand to her forearm. "I'm told I'm a good listener, so if you ever feel like getting it out. . . ."

A wise comeback hung on the tip of her tongue. But then something she couldn't identify, but that she'd kept locked in a dark part of her with the other things she didn't want to acknowledge, escaped. She looked at him for the first time since he'd come home. Really looked at him. His expression held no condemnation, just compassion and understanding. She felt like she could talk to him. But she held back. Maybe someday. Maybe never. But it was nice to know that he'd offered.

She smiled. "Thanks. I'll remember that."

Luc sat in the rocker for a while after Mandy went into the house. He'd spent a lot of years reading the faces of the kids who'd been sent to his office for one reason or another. That expression and the verbal evasions were all too familiar to him. There was no doubt in his mind that Amantha James was hiding something.

Oddly, he wanted to relieve her burden, hold her and tell her everything would be okay. Protect her from any pain and hurt.

Now, where in blazes had that come from?

Rather than think about what had prompted the new and unnerving emotions concerning Mandy, he rose and went into the house. Just inside the door, he could hear raised voices drifting up the hall from the family room. He caught sight of Mandy standing just outside and to the left of the family room door, eavesdropping on the conversation. When she saw him, she placed a finger over her lips

As he drew closer, the voices became more distinct. One of them was Shannon's, and the other was one with which he was very familiar. Jeb Tanner.

"It's not like the thing is alive, Shannon."

"Can't Mr. Michaels and this Mandy

person watch the baby for you?" This female voice was familiar as well, but Luc couldn't put a name with it.

"No, they can't. I told you. I'm the only one who can see to the baby."

"Stop saying that. It's a toy, for God's sake, not a baby. Get real." Jeb's voice had gained in volume and impatience. By the sound of it, he was quickly losing his temper. Then in a calmer, but obviously forced voice, Jeb said, "Are you coming to the dance with us, or are we going without you?"

Silence.

"I can't." Tears filled Shannon's voice. "I'm sorry, Jeb, please don't be mad at me."

"Come on, Darcy. We better leave Shannon to her *mommy* duties."

Seconds later Jeb Tanner and Darcy Williams hurried past Luc and out the front door without even a hello in acknowledgment. They were quickly followed by Shannon, who was holding Joey by one arm. The wail of the *robo* baby echoed through the hall as she ran up the stairs to her room.

Luc glanced at Mandy, expecting to see triumph in her face. Instead he saw a sadness that tore at his heart. "What was that all about?"

Mandy walked into the family room and

flopped down on the sofa. Luc followed. "Jeb and Darcy are going to the Fall Festival dance at the church, and they wanted Shannon to go, too."

"How did they know where she was?"

"Seems they overheard Asa Watkins talking to his wife on the phone." Mandy's derisive tone closely resembled Luc's when he talked about the School Superintendent.

Luc sighed. "Those kids will talk, and, if Laureene Talbot gets ahold of this information, it'll be all over town . . . with her usual embellishments. So much for keeping it under wraps."

And so much for keeping his job.

CHAPTER 7

That evening Mandy stood in the doorway
to the family room staring at the back of
Luc's head as he watched a baseball game
on the TV, the remote resting in his right
hand. Periodically, he would voice his
opinion, sometimes in colorful terms, of an
umpire's call or the ineptitude of a player to
catch or hit the ball. Obviously, he was
totally absorbed in the action taking place
on the big screen and unaware of her presence.

She wished she had something to occupy
her to the extent that she could block
everything out. But she didn't. Ever since
their conversation on the porch earlier that
day, Mandy could think of nothing except
Luc's offer to listen.

Over the years, people — friends, neighbors, teachers, social workers, the police —
had laughed at her, taunted her, gave her
condescending attention, and even pre-

tended to care only to prove they didn't. Never, in all that time, had anyone sincerely offered to listen, really listen . . . until Luc. Not that she expected him to shower her with sympathy. That wouldn't change the past. Besides, she couldn't stand any more sympathy. His feeling bad for her didn't change her past.

She slipped into the room, still indecisive about what she would do or say now that she was here, and took a seat next to him on the big sectional. Finally, she decided that if she did tell him about herself, it might serve to help him to better understand why getting the baby simulators into the classes would be beneficial, and why it meant so much to her. If she could accomplish that, it would be worth pulling her dirty laundry out of the box in which she'd kept it hidden for so many years.

But how in blazes did one start a conversation like that? Perhaps something along the lines of . . . *So, Luc, let me tell you about my crappy childhood.* She glanced at him. He was so immersed in the game that she wasn't sure he'd even detected her presence. Bottom-line was, no matter how she initiated the conversation, first she had to drag his attention away from the baseball game.

"Good game?" she asked conversationally.

"It would be if they'd get their heads out of their —" He turned to her, his face creased in a sheepish grin. "Sorry. I get too wrapped up in the game sometimes." His smile deepened, and Mandy's heart leaped. "Where's Shannon?"

"She went upstairs early. Between you and me, I think she's exhausted from getting up with Joey last night and plans an early bedtime."

Luc nodded, but made no comment and went back to watching the game.

Mandy sat silently staring at her folded hands, wondering how to divert the attention of someone so engrossed in a baseball game. The crack of the ball hitting the bat drew her gaze to the screen. As a runner crossed over the little white object in front of the man dressed in padding and a face mask, the crowd went crazy.

"Yes! Finally," Luc yelled, punching the air with his fist.

"Does that mean he got a touchdown?" She wasn't so ignorant of the sport that she didn't know a touchdown from a homerun, but that should get his attention.

The screen went black. Luc laughed out loud, then laid the remote on the coffee table and turned to her. "I can see I'm going to have to educate you in the American

131

male's favorite pastime. First of all, they score touchdowns in football. That was a homerun." Wide-eyed, she feigned understanding and nodded. He shifted his position to look directly at her. "Secondly, it was rude of me to ignore you in favor of the game."

Mandy was stunned. Sports had never been an interest of hers, but she knew enough about men and their favorite teams that little if anything came between them and a game. This man was obviously an unusual guy. Little things about Luc that she could appreciate were piling up faster than she could count. In the process, the wall she'd kept around herself for years was showing signs of crumbling. The realization sent a shock wave through her, followed by a chill of fear. That wall had been her protection against relationships for so long, and without it she'd be left vulnerable.

As with most things in her life that she found troubling, she tucked it away until later when she could think it through to a solution. "Don't let me interrupt. Please, go ahead and watch the game."

He grinned. "I can catch the score on the news later. Besides, my team was losing miserably. I'd rather not be witness to the slaughter." He stood. "It's beautiful evening. How would you like to take a walk down by the lake with me?" He held out his hand.

"I'd like that." Without thinking, she slipped her hand in his.

When her skin made contact with his, she had to catch her breath. Immediately, as if burned, she let go and then quickly preceded him out the door, her heart pounding so hard, it would be a miracle if it didn't fly right out of her chest.

As they walked along the shore of the lake, Mandy started second-guessing this idea. The setting came right out of a romantic, Hollywood chick-flick. The air was cool, yet not so cool that she needed a sweater. The smooth, moonlit lake stretched out before them like black silk swathed in streaks of liquid silver. A huge yellow moon hung in the sky surrounded by a faint sprinkling of sparkling stars. A soft breeze ruffled the trees. And a man, who was becoming far too important in her life, walked so close beside her she could feel his shoulder brush hers.

Talk about playing with fire!

For a long time they walked in silence. Soon they were far enough from the house that all she could see was the faint glow of light from Shannon's bedroom window. Joey must be awake.

Luc leaned close to her. "Let's sit and talk."

She started, then nodded. "Okay."

He cupped her elbow and guided her toward a large outcropping of rocks positioned so close to the shore that she could hear the water lapping gently against them.

Mandy boosted herself up on the biggest rock and turned so her feet dangled over the water. Luc sat beside her close enough that their thighs almost touched. Again, silence prevailed.

Mandy glanced up to see a shooting star streak across the night sky. "Look, a shooting star. Make a wish." She closed her eyes and wished her life had been different. Maybe then she could trust these feelings she was having for Luc and allow herself to follow wherever they led. But that was not gonna happen. She couldn't change what had already been. So the wish was wasted.

"I know what you wished for," Luc said, his voice deep and too near her face.

She turned to him in surprise. "You do?"

"Yes. You wished to win this test."

Mandy laughed. "You couldn't be farther from the truth."

"No? Then what did you wish for?"

134

"If I tell you, it won't come true." But then it wouldn't anyway. Besides, hadn't she been searching for a way to tell him about her childhood? Perhaps the heavens had provided the perfect opening. As if in answer to her unvoiced question, another star shot across the sky. Still she couldn't bring herself to start divulging her childhood.

"My turn to wish." He closed his eyes, then opened them and turned to her. "Want me to tell you what I wished for?" A tiny smile teased at the corner of his mouth.

How she loved his smile. It spread through her like sunshine, leaving behind warmth and . . . What? Finding no answer, she allowed the pleasant rush of emotions to wash over her. Some of the tension left her body. "If you want to, but remember, it may not come true if you do."

"I wished that you'd tell me why winning this test is so important to you."

She hesitated, staring deep into his eyes. "Were you being straight with me?" Studying his moonlit expression closely, she saw sincerity and caring reflected back at her. "Are you really a good listener?"

Instantly, his expression grew serious. "Absolutely. It's part of my job to be one."

Still she hesitated. Finding the words to

tell him something she'd kept hidden away deep inside for so long wasn't coming easily. Avoiding the subject altogether had been much simpler. But, she'd opened the door, and now she had to step through it.

She stared out over the lake, took a deep fortifying breath and began to talk. "I'm the product of a single parent home. I don't know who my father is, and my mother never saw fit to share that information with me . . . if she even knew. However, she wasn't a bit backward about reminding me on a daily basis, either with words or attitude, that I'd ruined her life, and that she wished I'd never been born."

She glanced at Luc out of the corner of her eye. His brows were drawn together in a frown, but he said nothing. Was the frown distaste? Disgust? Thoughtfulness? She couldn't tell, so she plunged on.

"Until I was eighteen, I lived in the poorest section of town, which teetered on the edge of squalor, and learned very early how to survive on my own. My mother made what few dollars we had by. . . . Let's just say she was employed in the world's oldest profession. Most of what she made went to buy her cigarettes and booze. My clothes came from the local thrift shop or church sales. My mother didn't cook, so my meals came from anywhere I could find food. Sometimes, after I got older and was able to get a part-time job, I bought groceries and cooked for both of us."

Luc drew in a sharp breath. "My God."

She turned to him. "I'm not telling you this for sympathy. Believe it or not, I do have a purpose."

"I'm listening." He smiled. What she saw in his eyes was definitely not sympathy, and a blanket of warmth slid over her chilled body.

"I don't want any other child or teenage mother to go through what my mother and I did. I don't hate her. She had no resources, no family support, no idea about what to do with a baby. But, she shouldn't have been in that situation to begin with. She never should have had a child. At least not at such a young age and with no idea of how to handle it. Perhaps, if someone had shown her the lifetime consequences of a few hours in the backseat of a car, she wouldn't have risked it."

He laid a hand on her arm. "I totally agree and have the utmost compassion for you and her, but I have to say that I'm very glad she had you."

Mandy stiffened and didn't know what to say. Tiny prickles of pleasure danced up her arm from where his hand lay. Something she couldn't put a name to filled his deep voice and wrapped around her like a warm breeze on a cold night. The world seemed to shrink down to this rock on the edge of the lake and just the two of them.

The silence that had fallen between them was broken by the hooting of a big barn owl perched in a tree just behind them. As they turned in unison to look at it, it spread its wings wide and flew over their heads, then disappeared into the darkness.

Luc glanced after the retreating bird and laughed. "I think he agrees, and you can't argue with the ancient wisdom of an owl."

Mandy found herself smiling. "Anyway," she went on, "the reason I'm telling you this is so you'll better understand why I'm so passionate about getting the baby simulators into the family planning class. No teen should have their life stolen from them because they're too immature to understand the long-term consequences of their actions. And no child should have to suffer simply because they were born at the wrong time." She finally stopped talking and looked at Luc for a reaction. "This is probably difficult for you to really understand. You must have had a much different childhood."

Luc released her hand, stood and then

walked to the edge of the lake. "I had clothes on my back, three good meals a day and a roof over my head."

Mandy frowned. What an odd way to describe his childhood. All material things. He'd said nothing about his parents. Maybe he didn't have any. "Were you an orphan?"

He laughed sarcastically. "No. Not really."

Not really? What did that mean?

"I don't understand." She waited for Luc to explain.

He shook his head and came back to the rock and sat down beside her. How could he complain when he'd had everything a kid could ask for: all the latest toys, good, nutritious meals, a wonderful education, clean, new clothes, and homes that were more than comfortable even if they were scattered all over the country? She'd lived without all these things.

However, from what she'd said, they did have one thing in common . . . neither of them had had the love and affection of caring parents. And, in the end, being deprived of that made all the rest insignificant.

Just then, his cell phone rang. He pulled it from his pocket, flipped it open and glanced at the illuminated screen. Asa Watkin's number. The very last person he wanted to talk to now. He closed it and replaced it in his pocket.

Though not taken, the call gave birth to a vivid reminder of his deal with Asa. Suddenly, what Luc was trying to do so he could keep his job left a very sour taste in his mouth. He was sure that very soon he'd have to make a choice between his settled lifestyle, his job and the welfare of the teens in his charge. And now he realized that if he made the wrong decision, he'd lose Mandy, and that tore at him in a very unexpected way.

CHAPTER 8

For a long time Luc said nothing more, just gazed silently out at the lake, enveloped in memories of a loveless childhood. The nights his nanny, and not his mother or father, had read bedtime stories to put him to sleep. The holidays when his parents had been *too busy* for him to come home from military school. The meals he'd eaten alone in a big empty dining room, because his father was in some far-flung country and his mother had some charity event she just *had* to attend.

Still, he'd had the nanny, the home and the meals. Mandy hadn't even had that much. So, in comparison to her young life, how did he have the right to complain that his childhood had been so terribly deprived?

"You could have taken that phone call." She smiled at him. The moonlight caught in her hair and eyes. For a moment, Luc could not look away.

He finally shook his head to dislodge the varied emotions cascading through his mind and body. "It wasn't important."

He shook off the guilty feelings the phone call had elicited, and as if by an unseen magnet, his gaze veered back to the woman beside him. She was gazing out over the lake now, and the moonlight illuminated her face, outlining the curve of her cheekbone and fullness of her lips. The beams seemed to become trapped in her hair, bringing to life the red highlights. Her face had an aristocratic quality that belied her impoverished upbringing and her down-to-earth personality. The way she held her chin high, as if fending off anything life could throw at her, told of her strength of character. The unwavering way her gaze met and held the person on whom her attention was focused, gave testimony to her sincerity.

All in all, she was the loveliest woman Luc had ever seen, both inside and out. So why wasn't she married? Or, at the very least, why didn't she have a boyfriend? Then again, he knew very little about Amantha James. Maybe she did.

How foolish. Of course, she did. A woman as lovely as she was must have men chasing her down at every turn. Luc found he didn't really like that idea one bit.

"So, who is he?" The question slid past Luc's lips almost before it formed in his mind.

Mandy turned to him, surprise reflected in her eyes. "Who?"

"The man in your life. You're far too lovely not to have been snatched up by some man."

A slight hint of embarrassment colored Mandy's laughter. "Afraid not."

It was his turn to be surprised. "Really?" He'd been so sure she had someone. Oddly, the idea that she didn't pleased him.

"My job keeps me way too busy for relationships. The teens I oversee need me, and I need to be able to give them my full attention. There's no place in my life for men and. . . . Well, let's just say I can't allow distractions."

His elation plunged into gloom. He heard the words she spoke aloud, but what he also heard was what she didn't say. Life with her single mother had turned her bitter on the subject of men and family and perhaps, even love.

She swiveled on the rock and faced him. "What about you? Anyone special?"

Having the tables turned on him left Luc speechless for a moment. He scoured his brain for a good reason that he was still single and, for the most part, dateless. "I guess, like you, my career has always taken center stage for me. When I became a principal, I vowed to do my very best for the kids who were looking to me for guidance. That takes time and devotion to my work." Not a lie.

She frowned. "Then why are you against introducing something into your school that will prevent teenage pregnancies?" She crossed her arms and began rubbing the exposed flesh, presumably to warm her chilled skin.

Although by now he knew Mandy's tendency to say what she was thinking, the question came at him like an unexpected blow to his gut. No way could he tell her about the unorthodox deal he'd made with Asa Watkins to keep his job. To appease his own conscience he told himself it would do the kids little good if he lost his job and had to leave Carson. For his explanation to her, he chose evasion.

"It's a long, uninteresting story. And it's getting late. It's also getting too chilly to be sitting out here without a coat. Let's go inside and get some hot coffee." He slid from the rock and held out his hand to her.

Mandy glanced at the moonlit face of her watch. She'd hardly consider seven fifteen

144

late, but nevertheless, she took his hand. Again, when his flesh touched hers, that tingle ran up her arm. But this time she was too busy trying to sort through his evasion to her question to think about anything else.

Long and uninteresting didn't do it for her. So, what was Luc hiding?

Once inside, Luc, who'd passed on the coffee and opted for a cold beer and a return to the Yankee game, had seemed very eager to leave her company. After retrieving a beer from the kitchen, he retired back to his position in front of the TV and left her standing in the hallway. As he walked away, his cell phone rang again. Stopping mid-stride, he pulled it from his pocket. After glancing at it, he closed it, did something with the side of it and then shoved it back in his pocket and disappeared inside the den.

Mandy wondered who it could be that was being so persistent, and he didn't seem to want to talk to, but she quickly pushed that aside and instead concentrated on the way he'd evaded her question. As a social worker she recognized the same signs in Luc that she'd seen many times when parents scooted around what was really happening in their homes. But why was Luc evading her question?

Unfortunately, try as she might, she could come up with no logical reason why, if he'd sworn himself to doing his best for the kids under his guidance, he would not share his reasoning for keeping the baby simulators out of the school. Unless. . . .

She recalled Asa Watkin's smarmy smile and covert glances at Luc at the school board hearing. Had Asa gotten to him? Could he be doing this because Asa had somehow threatened him if she got the simulators into the school? It seemed the only logical explanation for why a man, who cared so much about the students, would fight so hard to prevent implementing something of such benefit to them.

At the same time, she was sure Luc didn't impress her as the type of man to be bamboozled into doing something he didn't want to or that went against his ethics. So what was it?

When a knock sounded on the front door, she pushed aside her dilemma for the moment. After opening the door, she found Catherine Daniels standing on the porch.

"Hello, Catherine. Come in." She laughed, hoping to hide her embarrassment. "Listen to me playing the hostess. It's your house. You don't need an invitation."

"Hello, dear. On the contrary, as long as

you and Luc are here, I consider it your home. So your invitation is quite appropriate," she said as she stepped inside. "Speaking of Luc, is that a baseball game I hear?" She peeked around the corner of the den door and grinned. "I knew Luc would find that TV too tempting to resist."

Mandy forced a smile. "He's been glued to the baseball game all evening." Catherine had no need to know about their intermission by the lake. "What brings you here?"

"Let's go sit in the kitchen, and, if you have some already made, we can talk over a cup of coffee." Without waiting for Mandy to answer, she led the way to the back of the house and into the spacious kitchen.

When they both had a mug of coffee, they carried them to the breakfast nook and sat facing each other.

Catherine added cream to her coffee and stirred. "I came by for two reasons. I want to take Shannon shopping tomorrow, and I also wanted to know how she's doing with . . . uh . . . Joey."

Mandy sipped her coffee and set the cup aside. "I'll call Shannon down here in a moment, and we can check the baby's care monitor on my laptop. But first let's discuss this shopping trip. I'm going to give Shannon a budget. The money will come from the cash the school board allotted us for this project. She is not allowed to go over the amount I designate. I'm also going to have her make a list of things that Joey needs — diapers, formula, etc. She is to get these things first. Whatever is left, she can spend on herself, and you are not to supplement her money." Catherine frowned. "She has to learn that when you have a baby, his needs come before a new blouse or a new pair of shoes or a ticket to the latest movie, and there's not always going to be someone there to dole out more money when she runs out."

For a moment, Catherine looked taken aback, then comprehension shown on her face, and she nodded. "I understand. You can count on me. I'm just as eager for Shannon to see what a burden a baby can be at her age as anyone is."

Anyone but Luc, Mandy amended. She wouldn't say anything to Catherine about her conversation with Luc and his sidestepping an answer to her question.

"What's going on?" Both women looked up to find Shannon standing in the kitchen with Joey cradled in the crook of her arm. She looked a bit tired, and the faint evidence of loss of sleep was beginning to show beneath her eyes. Her hair, which had been stylishly and neatly arranged when Mandy first met her, was now pulled haphazardly into a ponytail with wisps that had escaped hanging listlessly around her face.

"Your grandmother came by to see if you'd like to go shopping tomorrow."

The tiredness seemed to vanish from Shannon's face. Her eyes lit with the eagerness that any young teenage girl would display at the prospect of a shopping trip. "Really?"

Catherine rose and hugged her granddaughter. "Yes, really. I'll pick you up right after lunch, and we'll drive into Charleston to the mall."

"You'll need to make a list to take with you of the things Joey needs." Mandy watched the young girl's reaction to her announcement. The light of excitement in Shannon's eyes dimmed just a fraction. "But right now, your grandmother would like to see how you're doing caring for Joey."

Mandy took the baby simulator from the girl and laid it face down on the table, then set up her laptop beside it. She opened the snaps down the back of the sleepers and hooked Joey up to her laptop. Seconds later, the screen displayed the information about his care.

"Looks like you're doing very well except

for the other day when you had visitors and this one spot this morning." Mandy pointed to the screen where a graph had appeared and showed a slight dip around seven a.m.

"I was in the shower when he started to cry, and I didn't hear him until I shut off the water." Shannon looked worried, but she'd skipped over any explanation about the day Jeb had come to ask her to the dance.

Mandy disconnected Joey and then re-snapped his sleepers. She closed the laptop and then handed the baby to Shannon. "No problem. Even real moms need to take a shower."

A sigh of relief escaped the teen. "There's one problem about tomorrow. I don't have a car seat for Joey, so I can't take him with me. Who's going to take care of him?"

Catherine tightened the arm around Shannon's shoulders. "What kind of great grandmother would I be if I didn't come equipped with a car seat for the . . . for my great grandchild?"

That was the second time Mandy'd heard a hesitation in Catherine's voice when speaking about the baby simulator. Obviously, thinking of the simulator as a real baby was more of a problem for Catherine than it was for Shannon.

"Great." The one word spoke volumes about Shannon's disappointment.

From her reaction, Mandy surmised that the young girl had been hoping to get away from her mommy duties for a while. Something Catherine appeared to have noted in Shannon's changed demeanor as well.

The older woman linked her arm with her granddaughter's. "Why don't we go upstairs and get caught up?"

"Sure." Lips pursed with continued disappointment at not being able to leave Joey home, Shannon turned and left the room with Catherine following closely behind.

As she watched them go, Mandy suddenly remember the request she'd made of Becky to help her find Catherine's daughter. It had only been a few days, but she was curious to know if Becky had made any progress in locating the woman.

She glanced down the hall to make certain she was not going to be overheard. Catherine and Shannon had disappeared up the stairs, and the sound of the baseball game still emanated from the den.

A loud cheer of "Way to go, Posada!" assured her that Luc was still riveted to the TV.

The office had been closed for hours, so she dialed Becky's home phone number.

A male voice answered. "Hello."

"Hi, Nick. It's Mandy. Is your wife around?"

"She sure is. Hey, sweetie, Mandy's on the phone," she heard him call out.

While she waited for Becky to take the phone, Mandy thought about the wonderful relationship her boss had with the man she'd married. All one had to do was look at them when they were together to understand the kind of enduring, unconditional love they had for each other. Maybe it was possible to have a lasting relationship with a man, a man who would always be there for you to help carry the burdens, celebrate the joys and love without question. A vision of Luc as they sat beside the lake that night slipped into her mind.

She shook her head to dislodge her foolish thoughts. Maybe it was possible for anyone else, but not for her.

Seconds later, Becky took the phone. "Hi, Mandy. What's up?"

"Nothing critical. I was just wondering if you'd found anything out about where Catherine's daughter is yet."

CHAPTER 9

Mandy glanced down the hall leading from the kitchen to make certain she wouldn't be overheard. The last thing she needed was Catherine, Shannon or Luc listening to her end of the conversation with Becky about Catherine's illegitimate daughter's whereabouts.

"We haven't found anything definitive yet," Becky went on, "but I have some pretty strong leads from the info you gave me. It's gonna take a while, Mandy. It's only been a few days, and you know as well as I do that you can't rush this."

Mandy turned to gaze wistfully out the window at the moonlit lake. "I know. I guess I'm a little anxious. I'd love to be able to do this for Catherine."

"I know, and so would I, but you need to be patient. And don't forget, the daughter will be in her early fifties. She probably has a family and a life, and she may not even want to know about her birth mother."

"I understand all that, and, if she doesn't want to meet her birth mother, then we won't tell Catherine that we found Hope. But if she does, then I want to give her that opportunity and Catherine, too."

The sound of a slightly impatient exhale came through the phone from Becky's end. "I'll keep trying to find her, but in the meantime, you need to give me the time to do the digging. Now, try enjoying your time off for a change and stop worrying." A pause.

Enjoy her time off? How could she do that with Shannon and Joey to worry about, not to mention the failure or success if this project, and on top of that, now she had a totally unwanted attraction to a man who was quickly becoming the center of her emotional life.

"Mandy? You hear me?"

Mandy sighed. "Yes, I hear you. I suppose if Catherine has waited this long, I can, too," she finally said, completely jumping over the *enjoy your time off* part.

"Hey, Becky! You still on the phone?" Nick's voice rang out in the background.

"That's my girl. Nick's calling. I need to run. We're having a late dinner on the patio, and my food's getting cold. Night."

"Night, and, Becky . . . thanks." Mandy hung up the phone.

"What's Catherine waiting for?"

Mandy froze. She turned very slowly. Luc stood in the kitchen doorway, a crushed beer can in his hand. How long had he been there? How much had he heard?

"Well, what's she waiting for?"

"I . . . uh . . ." She looked at the floor and floundered around in her head for something, anything to cover for what she and Becky had really been talking about.

"Let me help you. Can it be finding her daughter?"

Her gaze jumped to his. The anger in the straight line of his mouth and the pulsing muscle in his jaw told her he had heard far too much and had taken it the wrong way.

"I —"

He held up his hand. "Don't bother explaining. I've heard enough to get the basics. You're using Catherine's daughter to butter her up so you can win this . . . this . . . whatever you want to call it."

"That's not true. You're making assumptions from hearing one end of a private conversation." How could he think she was so underhanded that she'd do this for any reason but to see Catherine reunited with a child she'd lost fifty some years ago?

155

He stalked to the trash and threw the beer can into the container with undue force, then turned on her. "I'm not stupid. Don't you think I know that if you find her daughter that that's a point for you . . . a big point?"

Her own anger came to a simmering edge. "I didn't know we were earning points in this. And what about you? What's going on between you and Asa Watkins?"

His mouth fell open.

"I thought I had it figured out, and your reaction just confirms my suspicions, so there's no sense denying it. I remember how he looked to you for confirmation at the school board meeting, and how quickly you deferred to his opinions. I also know he's your boss and has a lot of pull with the school board. All that adds up. He's threatened your job, hasn't he?" She glared at him. "No need to answer that. I'm not stupid either, Luc."

Luc didn't know what to say, so he said nothing, neither confirming nor denying her assertion. They glared at each other like a couple of alley cats ready to do battle over a piece of fish. Neither said anything, but the look she cast his way spoke volumes. The silence stretched out into minutes.

She had indeed figured it out, and pretty

accurately at that. How could he deny it? And she probably wouldn't believe him if he told her that he wasn't so certain about allowing Asa to use him as his pawn any longer. He chose diversion.

"You're changing the subject." He flung open the refrigerator, extracted another beer and popped the top, not because he wanted another beer, but it gave him more time to think. After slamming the refrigerator door, he turned back to Mandy, his mouth open for another retort. Thankfully, he was rescued from having to further this discussion.

With a frown knitting her brows, Catherine stepped into the kitchen and threw both of them a disapproving glare. "What on earth are you two yelling about? I'm sure they can hear you on the other side of the lake."

Luc snapped his mouth shut and glanced at Mandy. She sent him a pleading look, then turned away and began rinsing a few dirty dishes that had been left on the counter and putting them in the dishwasher. Did she really think he'd spill everything to Catherine? She may think him low, but she couldn't think he was that bad. Still, she'd left him with the task of making some kind of explanation to Catherine.

A loud cheer coming from the TV in the den gave him an idea. "It's nothing, really. Mandy doesn't think the Yankees have a chance at the World Series, and I do." He forced a lopsided grin. "You know how us guys can get when it comes to our team."

Catherine shook her head. "No, I'm afraid I don't. My husband never followed team sports. His passion centered strictly around sailing. The one sporting event that worked him into a state of extreme excitement was the America's Cup Race." She picked up her purse off the table, then walked toward the door and stopped. "I'll pick Shannon up right after lunch tomorrow, if that's okay."

"That's fine," Mandy said without turning around. Catherine threw one last questioning look at Luc, then Mandy, then shook her head and left the room. Luc glanced at Mandy's stiff back and followed Catherine down the hall as far as the den. But even after he'd seated himself in front of the TV, he couldn't get his mind off what had happened in the kitchen.

Mandy had guessed his role in this experiment, and sooner or later he'd have to admit to it. Given her reaction without proof, he could just imagine what it would be when he confirmed her suspicions. Asa Watkins

158

had not only managed to involve Luc in his scheming, he'd also managed to drive a wedge between Luc and the only woman he'd felt anything for in years.

Luc left the house early the next morning. He had no desire to face Mandy across the breakfast table. Besides, he had things he could be doing in his office, and he wanted to pick up and deliver the papers for Alyce Walker to apply for her GED courses. As he drove toward town, he thought about his outburst the evening before when he'd overheard Mandy's phone conversation. Now that he could reflect on his rash reaction, he had to admit that she'd been right. It had been grossly unfair of him to judge her motives as the result of hearing one end of a conversation.

And now, in the clear light of day, he had to wonder if his own sense of guilt had been reaching for a way to vilify Mandy's intentions and perhaps whitewash his own. If he'd given her time to explain why she was looking for Hope, and he'd had time to think about it, he knew that, unlike his own, her motives were probably honorable and compassionate.

He'd accused her of buttering up Catherine to win. But in the end, if this experiment was not successful, and the simulators did not get incorporated in the Family Planning classes, neither he nor Mandy would be the losers. His students, the ones he cared deeply about, both male and female, would lose.

The more he hashed it over in his mind, the worse he felt. By the time he reached the school parking lot, his self-evaluation had sunk to a disturbing low. Slowly, he grabbed his briefcase, climbed from his car, locked it and headed inside.

However, instead of diving into his work, he sat at his desk and stared out the window at the athletic field, a constant reminder of Asa Watkins' priorities. As Luc stared at the bright yellow goal post at the end of the field, he saw not a championship football team, but the face of Alyce Walker and her baby staring back at him. When extracurricular activities took precedence over the moral welfare and future well-being of his students, Luc saw clearly what his choice had to be and what he had to do. Once the decision was made, the weight on his shoulders lessened. Unfortunately, it did not ease entirely, and his voluntary destruction of a life he'd worked very hard to establish still dogged him.

He spent the remainder of the morning

and part of the afternoon catching up on the paperwork that had accumulated in his absence. The distraction proved helpful in releasing some of the tension that had gripped his neck and shoulder muscles over the past few days.

When he'd completed his work, he gathered the paperwork Alyce would need to apply and start earning her GED and left his office. As he approached his car, he heard the unmistakably, familiar purr of a high-powered car coming in his direction. His nerves instantly tightened into little knots of apprehension. Turning toward the sound, he spotted Asa Watkins' low-slung, silver Jaguar XJ pull into the space beside Luc's old, blue Toyota. The contrast between the two cars further underlined the difference between him and Asa.

The last person he wanted to see or talk to right now was the superintendent. Luc waited while Asa opened his door and unfolded his thick body from the slick leather driver's seat. He took his time closing the door, then adjusting the lapels of his expensive suit jacket, before striding toward Luc with his usual self-assured gait.

"Luc, my boy." He extended his hand.

Luc ignored the proffered hand. "Asa." The greeting emerged stiff and unfriendly.

"What brings you here?"

"Well, if you'd answer your phone, I wouldn't be forced to chase you down in a parking lot." He smiled, but it didn't soften the reprimand, or that he knew Luc was avoiding him.

"I don't understand why you even thought you had to *chase me down.*"

Again, Asa flashed that smarmy smile. "Now, Luc, do I really have to explain why I wanted to talk to you?" A predatory grimace replaced the smile. "So how are things going?"

"Exactly which *things* are you referring to?" Luc was not about to make this easy for Asa.

Asa shook his head and made a *tsking* sound. "Luc, if you insist on being difficult and evasive, I'll have to assume our . . . little understanding is null and void. That being the case. . . . Well, you'll leave me no choice, my boy."

Luc felt like the rope in a tug-o-war. He had to break away from one side or the other before his nerves snapped. It seemed to have come down to a choice between this overbearing jerk and the students. Anger, guilt, the bad taste in his mouth just talking to this man gave birth to or just human decency pushed Luc over the edge. For

Luc, the choice was clear.

"You know what, Asa? Assume whatever you want. This test will proceed without interference from anyone. Not from you, and certainly not from me. And the results will be whatever they will be." He opened his car door and threw his briefcase into the back seat. "Now, I have an appointment."

Before Asa could say another word, Luc got in, started the car, and backed out of the space, leaving the School Superintendent with his mouth agape in the middle of the parking lot, languishing in a cloud of exhaust fumes. As Luc reached the end of the parking lot, his cell phone rang. He opened it, glanced at the caller ID and mumbled, "Asa," then shook his head in disbelief. Snapping it shut, he tossed it onto the passenger's seat.

Luc arrived at Alyce Walker's house twenty minutes later. After removing the GED instruction sheet from his briefcase, along with a note telling her where to go and the schedule, Luc climbed the steps and knocked on the door. Seconds later, it swung open, and he came face to face with Granny Jo Hawks.

"Granny Jo. Nice to see you again."

"Well, hello, Luc. What brings you here?"

She glanced behind him as though looking for something or someone. "Mandy's not with you?"

"No, ma'am. I just came from the school." He held out the sheaf of papers. "I brought these by for Alyce. It's the application to apply for her GED."

"She's at work, but I'll be happy to give them to her." Then she laughed. "Pardon my bad manners. Come on in, and sit a spell."

For a moment, Luc considered turning down the invitation, but then he thought about going back to face Mandy. He wasn't ready for that yet. "Thanks. I'd love to."

He stepped through the door into the clean, but sparsely furnished room. The house was quiet. The baby must be sleeping. A partially-finished, crocheted afghan lay beside a worn, pine rocking chair and a wicker basket containing several balls of colorful yarn. Taking a seat on the sofa, he leaned back, feeling more relaxed than he had all day.

"So, you best explain this to me so I can tell Alyce when she gets home." Granny Jo motioned to the papers she'd placed on the coffee table.

Briefly, Luc explained that Alyce would have to apply to see if she was qualified to take the course and then the test to earn her GED. The course would be taught and the tests given at the high school.

Granny smiled and settled back in the rocker, picked up her crocheting and then gave the floor a slight shove with her foot to set the chair in motion. "Well, that seems simple enough. And I'll see to it that she goes through with this." Then she stopped the rocker's motion, laid the partially finished afghan in her lap and leaned forward. She placed a warm hand on Luc's forearm. "I can't tell you how much this means that you're taking an interest in her. Poor thing has felt deserted by the ones who should be caring most about her and sweet little Lili. The last months have been a hard road for her to walk, but she's getting by. She's a tough little lady, and she's going to be okay in the end." She shook her head, and her voice took on a sad tone. "It just breaks my heart that she's missing out on a good chunk of her life. She should be worrying about grades and dates and not formulas and diapers and making ends meet. But she planted the seeds, now she has to tend the garden. Even so, she deserves a better life than this, and if getting that sheepskin is the way to go, then I'm all for it."

Luc had known why he was doing this, but aside from it being a well-known fact in Carson that Granny Jo was a woman with a big heart, he had no idea why she had taken an inordinate interest in Alyce and Lili's welfare. However, since it really wasn't any of his business, he kept silent.

Then those wise, old gray eyes narrowed on him. "I expect you're wondering why I'm so concerned with what happens to Alyce and Lili." She leaned back, picked up her needlework and propelled the rocker back into motion. "Plain truth is, she's my great niece. My horse's behind of a nephew, her daddy, and his wife threw the poor child out when she told them she was in the family way, and Lili's daddy claimed he wasn't responsible." She took a deep breath. "The Walkers have always been an uppity family. Disowned me when I married my Earl and come here to live." For a moment, she got a hurtful look in her eyes, as though the pain still resided deep inside her.

Then she shook her head and went on. "No one would take Alyce in, so I did. But even though I begged her to come live on the mountain with me, she refused. Said she could make it on her own." Her chest puffed out. "And she has. But it's been hard on her. Poor thing has worked her fingers to the bone, but she manages to keep a roof over their heads, clothes on their backs and food in their bellies. And that little baby is surely loved by her momma. Can't ask for more than that."

Luc nodded his agreement. "I'd say she has a lot to be proud of. Being a single mom and the only bread winner at her young age had to be a gigantic task for her. It's good she had you to help out."

Granny Jo dismissed his praise with a wave of her hand. "No more than any Christian woman would do for her own blood." She pointed at the papers. "She needs to get her GED and then go on to something more so she can get a decent job and doesn't have to struggle so hard to make ends meet." Then she frowned and centered her inquiring, gray eyes on him. "Now suppose you tell me why you're going to such lengths to make sure Alyce gets her GED."

Why indeed. Luc hadn't really been absolutely sure until this moment. "Because I vowed, when I got my degree, that I would help any kid I could to get the best education and start in life that they could. Just because Alyce didn't attend Carson High doesn't negate that promise."

■ ■ ■ ■

On his way to the lake house, Luc thought about what he'd told Granny Jo and how it made the deal he'd made with Asa to keep the baby simulators out of the school look like the worst blatant betrayal of his vow. A good education meant a solid future for these kids, and just because Asa didn't want to take the money from his precious athletic budget didn't mean the kids should suffer by having their lives ruined. Mandy was right. They needed to know what they'd be sacrificing by having a child while they themselves were still children — the hardships, the long nights, the living hand to mouth, paycheck to paycheck.

It was at that moment that Luc cut all ties with Asa. If he had to move to a new town and start over, then so be it. He'd started a life from nothing once before. He could do it again. For the first time in days, Luc felt clean. The one thing that dimmed his pleasure in his decision was that leaving Carson meant leaving Mandy.

CHAPTER 10

That night Luc and Mandy walked a wide path around each other, speaking to each other only when necessary, neither of them able to find a way to break the icy barrier between them. Upon arriving back at the lake, Luc had gone directly into the den and switched on the TV. When he'd gone to the kitchen for a beer, he'd noticed Mandy out on the deck staring blindly at the lake. He'd assumed she'd stayed there until she'd been forced to come inside and start dinner.

Shannon had come home from shopping angry with Catherine and sporting an attitude because, after buying diapers and formula for Joey, she hadn't had enough money left to purchase a blouse she'd just "had to have." And, as instructed by Mandy, Catherine had not offered to supplement Shannon's money to make the purchase. Added to that was the embarrassment she'd suffered when Joey had launched into a screaming fit in the middle of the store, and, unable to quiet him, she and Catherine had been asked to leave. By the time the young girl had gotten home, she'd been tired, cranky and sullen.

Dinner that evening was, to say the least, an excruciating exercise in silence. Thick and uncomfortable tension had lain over the entire room like a suffocating blanket, leaving little inclination for conversation. Despite that, Luc had tried several times to initiate an exchange, but when all he'd gotten for his efforts were frowns and indecipherable grunts from Mandy and continual complaints about how unfairly she was being treated from Shannon, he'd fallen silent, too.

Following breakfast the next morning, Mandy reminded Shannon that Joey's clothes needed washing, and she should clean his corner of their room where she'd set up the nursery, including sanitizing his crib and washing all the bedding. Obviously unhappy with the task, Shannon nevertheless reluctantly shuffled off to do her chores.

By the time Luc put his dishes on the counter, Mandy had come to the conclusion that it was time to bury the hatchet. They each had their agenda as far as the simulators were concerned, and neither approved of the other's. So be it. Besides, she'd known they were on opposite sides of the fence going in to this, so why get all in a snit about Luc's attitude now? In a few days they'd have an answer. In the meantime, she'd talk to Luc and let the chips fall where they may. Perhaps they could at the very least get on speaking terms again.

Luc turned to go.

"Please don't leave. I'd like to talk to you, if you don't mind." She poured a cup of coffee for herself and set an empty cup out for him. "Let's go out on the deck. Shannon doesn't need to hear this conversation."

Without a word, Luc nodded, but didn't immediately follow her outside. "I'll be there in a minute. Just let me get a cup of coffee."

She just nodded and went outside, leaving the door open for him to follow. Taking a seat at the large, glass table, she set her cup in front of her and wrapped both hands around the hot mug. While she waited for Luc to join her, she looked out over the blue waters of Lake Hope.

For as far as she could see, the scene appeared like a serene picture straight off one of the postcards on the 2 for $1.00 rack in Keeler's Market. The autumn day had

171

dawned beautiful and clear. The lake was a smooth reflection of the blindingly blue sky and sparkled where the morning sun's rays danced off the few ripples in the surface. Bright oranges, yellows and reds painted the trees that filled the landscape on the lake's edge, where a beautiful male deer with an enormous rack of antlers drank from its waters. The rich aroma of pine and unique scents of autumn wafted to her on a crisp morning breeze. In the distance, the top of Hawks Mountain peeked above the treetops.

Mandy wished she felt as calm as the vista before her. She wrapped her arms around her chilled body, wishing she'd thought to grab her sweater. Her stomach churned with nervous tension. She combed her brain trying to find the right words to start this dreaded conversation. At last, Luc emerged from the house with his coffee in one hand and her sweater in the other.

"I saw this draped over the kitchen chair and thought you might need it." He placed the sweater around her shoulders and sat next to her. "You looked cold," he said in reply to her questioning glance.

Thoughtful as well as so handsome he took her breath away every time she saw him. She'd gotten used to her heart speeding up when he entered a room, but the bottomless feeling in her stomach that always accompanied it still put her off balance. Alarm bells went off in her head. Luc Michaels was becoming way too dangerous to her peace of mind and her vulnerable heart. Trying her best to ignore the emotions bombarding her, she smiled at Luc.

"I am chilly. Thanks." She drew the sweater around her body to cover her bare arms.

"So what's this talk we need to have?"

"It's about that argument we had —"

"No." He held up his hand to stop her from saying more. "Me first. I had no right to fly off the handle at you and make unfounded accusations just because I overheard one side of a phone conversation. You were absolutely right to get angry with me."

First the sweater and now this unsolicited apology?

Too stunned to say anything for a moment, Mandy could only gape at him. Finally, she cleared her throat. "I was right?"

"Yes, and I apologize. First, I shouldn't have been eavesdropping, and second, I shouldn't have accused you of anything without proof." Previously, his gaze had been directed at his coffee cup. Now, he raised it to meet hers. A hint of a smile teased at the corner of his mouth. "Am I forgiven?"

Even just the hint of his smile did something crazy to her insides. His expression reminded her of Davy Collins the day his wolf, Sadie, had charged into the Social Services office and scared two female clients half to death. Apologetic, but in some strange way a bit amused with himself. "Please say yes. I feel like a complete jerk."

Mandy swallowed. Her first impulse was to reach out to him, but she stopped herself with the reminder that she needed to keep distance between this man, whose mere presence had the ability to set her heart to racing out of control, and herself. At least until she could get control of her unpredictable emotions.

Instead, she balled her hands into fists, stood, moved to the porch rail, and then turned to face him. "Yes, you're forgiven, but I should apologize, too. I had no right to accuse you of the things I did, Luc." Then she smiled.

Her smile threw his thoughts into chaos. Luc looked away. *Now. Tell her she was absolutely right about his deal with Asa. Do it now,* a little voice whispered. But he couldn't. He couldn't bring himself to spoil their first moment of peace in days.

He rose and joined her at the railing, then covered her hand with his own. "So we're friends again?"

She glanced down at their hands and then smiled up at him and nodded. "Yup. Friends."

When she tried to pull her hand from his, he tightened his grip. For a moment, she resisted, then he felt a slight tightening of her fingers, as if she, too, didn't want to let go of him or the moment.

His gaze fastened on her lips as she'd said the words. Then it shifted to her eyes. "Good."

Had that been his husky voice? He didn't know for sure. What he did know was that he wanted to taste her mouth more than he wanted to take his next breath.

"Yes . . . good." Her whisper drifted away on the breeze. A dreamy expression filled her eyes.

The wind lifted a strand of her hair and laid it across her cheek. Unable to resist, Luc brushed it back behind her ear. Once he'd touched her, he couldn't seem to summon the will to break the contact. His hand rested against the cool skin of her neck.

Their gazes held. The sounds of nature welcoming the new day faded. Before he could stop himself, he leaned forward and touched her lips lightly with his. They were cool and inviting and tasted like the honey she'd had on her toast. But best of all, she didn't pull away.

She leaned toward him. A moan escaped from one of them. Luc wasn't sure who, nor did he care. Her arms circled his neck, and he pulled her against his chest. He'd never held a woman and felt like this before, like she belonged in his arms . . . in his life, in —

"Mandy!"

That sound of Shannon's strident voice from inside the house brought them back to earth. Mandy tore her mouth from his and sprang from his embrace. She moved quickly to the side of the porch closest to the open kitchen door, her eyes large and wary.

A yawning emptiness filled Luc's soul, and a knot of apprehension filled his throat. Wary? He struggled to understand. "Mandy, I —"

For a moment, she could do nothing but stare at Luc. Mandy didn't have a great deal of experience with the opposite sex, having devoted much of her life to her career, but what little she had left her totally unprepared to contend with what had just happened. Never had she felt with any other man what Luc had just brought to life in her. She'd always been careful not to get involved physically. But she knew for a certainty that if Shannon had not interrupted, she would have gone wherever Luc led her. No protests. No hesitation. Just blindly followed. And it scared her beyond explanation.

"Mandy, where are you?" Shannon called again. "I can't make the stupid washer work."

Mandy blinked, then turned toward the sound of Shannon's agitated voice.

"I'm out here on the deck. I'll be right there," she called, her tone husky and shaky. Then she swung back to face Luc, and in a low whisper said, "This can never happen again."

Lunch was as quiet as this morning's breakfast and the previous night's supper, but for totally different reasons. Luc was still puzzled about Mandy's reaction to their kiss. He knew she'd enjoyed it as much as he had by the way she'd responded. Yet, he could still recall the way she'd looked at him with that guarded expression, almost as though she was afraid of him, of what he might do . . . or had it been what *she* might do?

He studied her from across the table. She seemed more interested in rearranging her salad than anything going on around her, even though she'd barely touched a bite.

Shannon was in a snit again because Mandy had made her wash not only Joey's clothes but her own as well. She'd also told Shannon that from now on, she'd be helping to prepare all their meals and doing some of the housework. That had not set well with the teenager, who was beginning to show distinct signs of displeasure with her role as mother and housekeeper.

Luc said nothing. If she'd been living on her own with Joey, as Alyce was with Lili, then she would be the one to shoulder all the household tasks as well as caring for an infant. Allowing her to think otherwise would not only defeat the purpose for all this, it would also give her a false sense of what to expect as a young, single mother.

"I never have any time for myself. It's not fair," she'd wailed when told to clear the table and do the dishes. "You guys do whatever you want and go wherever you want, and I'm stuck here."

"We don't have a baby to care for," Luc reminded her. His statement had drawn a surprised look from Mandy, but she said nothing.

Shannon's only reply was to stick out her bottom lip, push her unfinished lunch aside and stomp from the room. Before she'd reached the first landing, Joey wailed loud and clear, but the sound of Shannon's bedroom door slamming muffled it. Mandy glanced at Luc, shrugged and left the room. Both she and Shannon had remained out of sight until late afternoon when they'd reappeared in the kitchen and began making dinner.

Now, all three were once more sharing a silent meal, for which no one appeared to have any appetite. Twenty minutes into the meal, Joey wailed out for attention. Shannon swore softly, threw down her fork and left the room in an angry huff.

Luc set aside his fork. He hesitated to speak to the uncommunicative Mandy, but his curiosity got the best of him. "Is it my imagination, or is he crying more often than before?"

"I reset the frequency of his crying yesterday. Babies get sick, and babies have bad days. She has to see that." Mandy never raised her gaze from her plate.

Pushing his plate to the center of the table, Luc rested his forearms on the placemat. "What's wrong? I thought we were friends again." Silence. "Is it what happened

179

on the deck this morning? If it is, I'm sorry it upset you, but I'm not sorry it happened."

Mandy threw him an indecipherable look, picked up her plate and went to the sink. She scraped the untouched contents down the drain, turned on the faucet and then switched on the garbage disposal. The grinding of the disposal seemed to magnify the wall Mandy had erected between them.

Luc followed her and turned off the disposal. "I'm not going away, and inserting that noise into our conversation will not end it." He took her shoulders and turned her toward him, then hooked his finger under her chin and raised it, forcing her to look at him. "What is it, Mandy?"

She glanced at him. Her gaze shifted to his lips. How very much she wanted to feel his kiss again, to — She sighed and removed herself from his grasp. Having him touching her did not help her vow to avoid a repeat of what had happened on the deck. It made it much too easy to remember their kiss and the way she felt in his arms, safe and secure for the first time in her entire life. But she'd also felt small and helpless, and that frightened her beyond words. How she wished she could react like any normal woman to a man's touch. But nothing in her life had ever been normal. Nothing. She couldn't allow one kiss to make her forget that.

In that fraction of an instant after Shannon had called to her and broken the spell of the kiss, Mandy had realized the danger she'd put herself in. Her heart had told her days ago that this man was becoming far too important to her, and she could only save herself by making sure nothing like that kiss ever happened again. Getting involved with any man had no place on her life's agenda. If her mother had taught her anything, it was not to trust a man. They always lied to you, and, in the end, they always let you down.

"This isn't about you, Luc. And it's not about a stolen kiss on the deck this morning. It's about me and the choices I've made for my life."

"And these choices don't include me personally? Or they don't include men in general?" Luc frowned down at her, managing to look hurt and sexy at the same time.

Mandy couldn't afford to react to either the hurt or the attraction. She couldn't afford to let Luc charm his way any further into her soul than he already had. She couldn't care for him. She just couldn't.

"It's a long story, and I'm not sure I'm ready to share it. I'm not sure if I ever will be, either, so please don't ask."

Before he could stop her, she whirled and left the kitchen and him standing beside the sink with the look of confused hurt deepening in his soft brown eyes. She lurched to a stop in the hall, leaned heavily against the wall, and squeezed her eyes shut. But she couldn't block out the way Luc had looked at her just before she fled. Like a little boy who'd been slapped by someone he trusted.

Luc wanted her trust, and she wanted to give it to him. But a person is only given a certain amount of trust, and she had given all hers away to a mother who didn't deserve it.

CHAPTER 11

In the following days, and much to Mandy's relief, an unspoken truce settled between her and Luc. He didn't ask any more questions, nor did he attempt to repeat the kiss, and she became less wary around him. Luc had stopped referring to Joey as *robo* baby, and their strange little household began to take on all the aspects of a real family, something Mandy had never experienced. The evenings especially had become a time when they would gather together in front of the TV and watch a movie or play a board game.

The one flaw in their otherwise content world was Shannon's growing discontent with being a mommy. She'd happily join in the games and watching TV, which was the only time she resembled a carefree teen. But when Joey's strident cry rang out, her smile would vanish, and the frown that Mandy had come to know so well, and that was so

183

unlike the happy, enthusiastic girl she'd first met, would transform the girl's face.

Mandy also noticed that it was taking the young girl longer and longer to quiet Joey's cries for attention, and she'd begun referring to Joey as *it* more often than she used the name she'd chosen so carefully for him. When Mandy had checked the monitor in the simulator, the demerits were alarmingly high, and the day she'd mentioned it to Shannon, she'd thrown down the laundry she'd been folding and ran from the room in tears.

Catherine had dropped by a few times and asked Shannon to go to lunch or shopping, but she'd refused. "It's not the same. I want to go out with my friends, not my grandmother," she'd snapped and left Catherine standing there with a helpless look on her face.

The tension between Mandy and Shannon peaked midweek when Mandy went to do her laundry and found the washer full of wet, musty baby clothes. Grabbing a handful of the wet garments, Mandy stormed into the kitchen where Shannon was eating lunch.

"Did you forget these?" She thrust the wet clothes at Shannon. "You're going to have to rewash them. The baby can't wear clothes that reek of mustiness."

Shannon laid down her sandwich and glared at Mandy. "Oh, yeah. Like it's going to catch some horrible disease and die." She frowned. "Helloooo. It's not a real baby. Geeze, Mandy." She went back to eating her sandwich.

"Maybe you missed the part where for all intents and purposes, Joey is real to you. He needs the same care as a real baby." Mandy threw the clothes on the table. "Rewash them."

Shannon pushed them away. Then, throwing down the remains of her sandwich, Shannon jumped to her feet. "You're not my mother, and he," she pointed an accusing finger at Luc, who had been standing silently nearby, "is not my father. So get off my back."

"You will not speak to Mandy like that, young lady." Luc's voice was hard and commanding.

Shannon glared at Luc and then stomped from the room and down the hall. The front door slammed behind her.

Mandy didn't know what to say. She stood open-mouthed staring at the empty doorway. A moment later, a hand touched her shoulder. She turned to find Luc standing close by her side.

185

"She'll cool down after she's had some time to think. In the meantime, why don't you take a drive into town and do the grocery shopping?" He handed her the list they kept hanging from a magnet on the refrigerator. It included bread, canned soup and cheese, but she could see in his eyes that he wasn't as concerned with the food as he was with her peace of mind. "You haven't been away from here in days. It'll do you good."

Mandy didn't think Shannon would cool down much, but he was right about needing time away from here. The tension between her and Shannon had become unbearable, and her nerves felt like elastic bands stretched to their limit. Shannon may have been learning what it was like to be a teenage mother, but Mandy was quickly learning what it was like to be the mother of a rebellious teen.

She looked up at Luc, and for a moment allowed herself to soak up the compassion in his expression. It worked on her taut nerves like a soothing balm. How was it he had the power to do that with just a look? Days of physical and mental fatigue caught up to her, and the urge to just lean against him and bask in that feeling of protective warmth and security almost overwhelmed her.

Maybe she'd been wrong not to trust him. She'd always measured all men by the unending stream of ne'er-do-wells that had paraded in and out of her mother's house when she'd been growing up. None of them had stayed longer than a few days, just enough time to get what they wanted from her mother with their smooth talking lies. And when each one left, her mother had turned to her pacifier, the bottle, and ranted on and on about how Mandy was ruining everything for her. But maybe Luc was different.

And maybe he's not.

Before she could do something she'd regret later, she moved away from his magnetic aura. With her nerves in bad shape and her mood even worse, she figured she was ripe for some serious sympathetic hugs.

She had to get out of there . . . and fast.

"I think I'll take your suggestion. I haven't been by the office for a few days either. I can do both while I'm out, but I shouldn't be too long."

He smiled, and that urge to be close to him came sneaking back into her mind. She pushed it away.

"Take as long as you need. I'll hold down

187

the fort."

Mandy sighed. "In the mood she's in," she motioned toward the doorway where Shannon had disappeared, "you'd better put on a suit of armor."

His expression changed from the light-hearted friend urging her to take time for herself, to the serious man who'd kissed her on the deck. "Don't underestimate my determination. When I put my mind to it, I can be a formidable opponent."

Mandy had the unmistakable and very uncomfortable feeling that he was no longer talking about the rebellious teen who'd just stormed from the room.

Not long after the sound of Mandy's car faded into the distance, Luc heard the back door close. He entered the laundry room and found Shannon throwing baby clothes into the dryer with a lot more force than necessary.

"Shouldn't you be rewashing them?" Silence followed, and Luc began to think she hadn't heard him, or had opted to ignore him.

"Probably." But she threw another handful of wet clothes in the dryer. "He doesn't get them dirty, so I don't see why they have to be washed anyway."

"Mandy's right, you know. If you want a baby, all this that you hate comes along with it." He leaned against the door frame and continued to talk, even though Shannon appeared to be ignoring him. "I understand your frustration and that you'd rather be out having fun with your friends. I wish you could be, too. But you chose this, just as you would have chosen to have a real child. Now, you have to stick it out and put up with the results."

Shannon whirled on him, tears glistening in her eyes, her pretty face contorted in anger. "If she'd just give me a break once in a while. But she's always on my case. Joey needs this. Joey needs that. I'm sick of him and her."

Teenagers. Luc sighed in frustration. "Then maybe you should give up on this and go home."

"Maybe I should."

"Or you could prove her wrong and stick with it."

"In your dreams." She glared at him, slammed the dryer door closed, jabbed the *start* button on the dryer, then stormed past Luc.

That certainly wasn't the reaction he'd been looking for. He wanted her to stay, to see it through, to fully understand what being a parent meant. Instead, he'd pushed her into giving up.

How do parents do it? Or was it perhaps different if it was *your* child and there was that deep love bond? He wouldn't know. He'd never experienced that connection with his parents.

He sighed and rubbed at a spot on his temple that had suddenly begun to throb.

Later that day, Luc, having given the teenager time to cool down, looked around briefly for Shannon. She was nowhere in the house. Shrugging, he decided she'd gone for a walk to calm down. He ran upstairs, checked on Joey, who was quiet in his crib, then Luc went back through the house to the kitchen, grabbed his coffee and took it onto the deck.

Once there, his gaze seemed to automatically go to one spot. For a long time, he stared at the railing where he and Mandy had kissed. Warm, sweet memories drove all thought of the teen from his mind. He ran his tongue over his lips, as though testing for remnants of the sweet honey he'd detected on her lips that day. Like the kiss, the honey had become a memory, but nevertheless, a sweet one. Along with that memory came the recollection of the expression on

190

Mandy's face just before she'd announced that they could never do that again.

At the time, he'd interpreted it as wary, but the more he thought about it, the more he thought it had been fear. But why? He'd never given her a reason to be afraid of him. And it certainly couldn't have been the kiss itself. Her response had more than proved that she'd enjoyed it as much as he had.

This woman that he was coming to care a great deal for was an enigma, a mixture of puzzle pieces, and none of them seemed to fit together to give him a true picture of the real person. And if her response to his questions earlier meant anything, it didn't appear as though she'd be sharing her secrets anytime soon . . . if ever.

But she'd never come up against a determined Lucas Michaels.

He'd perfected the art of wheedling things out of reluctant students. Certainly he could handle one social worker.

The sound of raised, but muffled voices coming from inside the house cut short Luc's musings. Had Mandy returned and gotten into it with Shannon again? He rose and went inside, preparing himself to step between them. As he walked toward the front of the house, the voices became more distinct and sounded as though they were

191

coming from Shannon's room, and none of them were Mandy's.

"That's not fair!" Shannon sounded like she'd been crying. "He knows why I'm doing this. It's for us. For him and me."

"I know, but he's changed his mind. He doesn't think it's a good idea anymore, Shannon." Luc didn't recognize the other female's voice. "I told him to talk to you, but he said he's done talking, and he's done waiting. If you don't show up tonight, he's going to take Jean to the dance."

Feeling a bit guilty for eavesdropping, Luc moved closer to the foot of the stairs.

"I can't. I have to take care of the baby. Why can't you understand that? Why can't he?" Shannon wailed, her voice thick with tears.

"Can't you leave it with them?"

Silence. Luc held his breath waiting for Shannon's reply. More silence. Then. . . .

"No. They can't do it. I'm the only one with a key to stop it from crying."

It. Not a good sign.

"Well, you better make a decision. I have to tell Jeb if you'll be meeting him or not."

Luc waited for Shannon's reply, but none came. All he could hear was the faint sound of someone crying.

Mandy entered the Social Services office and found Becky sitting at her desk talking to her grandmother, Granny Jo Hawks. When she walked in, their conversation stopped, and they both turned to her.

Becky looked very surprised to see her. "What are you doing here?"

"I needed to get away."

Granny Jo laughed. "Well, if that don't beat all. You had to get away from your getaway?"

Mandy realized what she'd said sounded strange. Since neither of them knew what she was really doing at the lake, she fumbled to explain what seemed to be an odd statement from someone supposedly on vacation. "I guess I'm just not used to having a lot of idle time on my hands."

"You have idle time with the beautiful lake out there? Seems to me you could find all kinds of things to do . . . swimming, boating, laying around in a hammock catching the sun." Granny Jo gave her one of those all-knowing looks of hers. "Now, suppose you tell us why you're really here when you should be enjoying your time off."

Mandy hesitated. How could she tell them

she'd come here hoping to escape a snarling teenager and a man who was carving his name on her heart?

"No need," Becky chimed in. "I know why she's here. She came to see if I've gotten any information about Catherine's daughter."

Relief flooded Mandy. Then what Becky had just said registered in her fried brain. "Becky!" Mandy couldn't believe she'd said that in front of Granny Jo when it was supposed to be their secret.

"Oh, child," Granny said, waving away Mandy's alarm with her hand. "Calm yourself. I've known about that girl for years. My Earl and Catherine's husband were best friends from kindergarten. He confided in Earl years ago that Catherine was searching for her daughter. Darn near broke up their marriage till she finally gave up." She smiled at Mandy. "Knowing your good heart, it doesn't surprise me that you've taken up the hunt."

Mandy relaxed. "You know this is not to leave here, right?"

"Won't come from my lips." Granny Jo made a motion as if closing an invisible zipper over her mouth. Then she shook a finger at her. "Just make sure Laureene Talbot doesn't get wind of it, and you'll be fine."

"She won't," Mandy assured her. Then she turned to Becky. "Have you found her?"

Becky grinned and nodded. "Yesterday. Funny thing is she's lived her whole life about forty miles from here in Madison."

Mandy couldn't believe it. Elation replaced all the tension stemming from her run-in with Shannon earlier. "That's wonderful!"

Instantly, Becky's smile evaporated. "Don't get too excited. There's one catch."

"Oh?"

"I'm afraid she doesn't want to meet Catherine."

"What?" Mandy couldn't believe that a child, no matter how old, would not want to know her birth mother. "Why not?"

"She says it's water over the bridge. She has a good life, a husband, two kids and three grandkids, and she doesn't want to disrupt their lives by bringing this stranger into it."

"Stranger? It's her mother, for heaven's sake, not some. . . ." At a loss for words, Mandy collapsed into a chair in front of Becky's desk. "But I —"

Becky leaned toward Mandy. She rested her arms across a folder that bore Catherine's last name. "We made a deal when I agreed to take this on. If the girl didn't want to meet Catherine, we'd drop it. I gave her Catherine's name and address, and if she changes her mind, that's totally her decision." Becky picked up the folder and stuck it in her top desk drawer. "Now, we . . . *you* need to drop it."

Reluctantly, Mandy nodded. "You're right. Consider it dropped." Deep inside, she said a silent prayer that this woman would change her mind.

Granny Jo rested her hand on Mandy's shoulder. "I'm sorry, child. I would have liked to see it end differently, too, but you have to respect the woman's wishes. And there are plenty of others out there who need you."

Mandy nodded and got up. "Well, I guess I'll get back to my *glorious* vacation."

She hugged Granny Jo and waved to Becky, then left the office, her heart as heavy as it had been when she'd arrived, but for a different reason.

When Mandy arrived back at the house, she sat in the car for a while, dreading going back inside and facing Shannon. Even though things seemed to be working out with Shannon and the simulator as Mandy had predicted, she wasn't at all sure her nerves could stand much more of the tension between them.

Thank goodness for Luc, who'd been acting as a buffer between them, which had surprised her. It seemed he'd had a change of heart concerning the simulators, but she didn't trust that it wasn't all just a front to throw her off guard. They only had a few more days before the decision would be made.

A few more days, and she'd never have to see Lucas Michaels again. The thought brought no joy, just a weighty sense of unbelievable sadness.

Mandy had just gotten out of the car when she caught the sound of Joey's wails coming from the house. Heaving a sigh that this probably meant another go-round with Shannon, she climbed the stairs and went inside.

It didn't take long for her to identify the direction from which the sounds were emanating. She set the single grocery bag containing the few non-perishables on the side table. Taking a deep, fortifying breath, she walked down the hall toward the back of the house and entered the TV room. What she saw brought her to an abrupt halt.

CHAPTER 12

Mandy peeked around the doorframe and watched in amusement as Luc paced back and forth with a crying Joey cradled in the crook of his arm. On the floor beside the sofa were several discarded diapers, evidently a valiant attempt to appease the simulated infant.

As if he held a real child, Luc talked to it in a continuous stream of placations designed to soothe the simulator and stop his cries. "It's okay, Joey. Your mommy will be back soon. You know, she didn't leave you because she doesn't care about you. Your mom is just tired and frustrated and wants to be a teenager for a while. Sometimes, mommies don't really like being mommies and being home all the time."

The desperation in Luc's voice brought a wider smile to Mandy's face. The endearing way he spoke to the simulator, the compassion in his voice all tugged at Mandy's already vulnerable emotions . . . especially where this tall, handsome man was concerned.

That reaction alarmed her. Why, when she'd sworn to steer clear of any relationships, had her heart made an exception for him?

Before she could come up with an answer, the baby stopped crying and made a sound like a hiccup. Although it appeared as though Luc's soothing tone had gotten through to the simulator, Mandy knew it wasn't because of anything Luc had said or done. She'd programmed the simulator to fuss and knew it would start crying again in a short time.

Feeling a bit guilty about eavesdropping, Mandy nearly stepped forward to make her presence known, but as if he didn't realize the baby had gone silent, Luc, with his back to her, continued to sway while he began talking again. However, his tone had changed from the soothing, sing-song cadence he'd first used with Joey to one tinged with anger.

"It's not just single moms who don't want their babies." He gazed out the window at the lake, but from his tone, something told her that he didn't see the beautiful vista before him, and that his sight was centered somewhere in the past . . . his past. "Sometimes, even grownup mommies would rather be out having fun than home taking care of their kids."

What really got to her was not the anger, but the way his shoulders drooped and the ring of sadness in his voice. His words had become personal. Suddenly, she felt as if she'd been listening in on a private conversation, one she had no right to hear. Mandy's humor at the situation she'd stumbled on dissipated.

Still, she remained out of sight, trying to get a grip on the way the pain in his voice cut deep inside her and brought forth a strong urge to run to him and wrap him in her arms. She wanted to make the hurt she'd heard in his voice go away, to see him smile that smile that made her knees go weak. But she held back.

Why? Was it just because she didn't want to intrude on a private moment? Or was it something more serious? For the first time, she found herself really assessing her feelings for this man.

At first it had been purely antagonistic. Luc had been an adversary. But little by little, she had come to see him not as the enemy, but just a man who didn't understand the significance of what she hoped to accomplish. Along with that, somewhere along the line, she'd opened her heart and allowed herself to care for him . . . too much. She'd allowed her heart to overrule her head, and now she found herself teetering precariously on the edge of the same situation her mother had been in when she'd let her hormones guide her actions. But was it just hormones, or was it something bigger? Was it love?

Unwilling to face that possibility, Mandy shook away her thoughts and concentrated on the man holding the simulator. What the situation boiled down to was that she had a choice to make. She could just stand there and eavesdrop, something that went against her nature. Or she could turn and walk away, something that went equally against her nature. Or she could go in there and help Luc.

Taking a deep breath, she stepped into the room. "Luc?" She looked around as though just realizing he was alone. "Where's Shannon?"

He spun around, obviously surprised by her appearance. "She took off with her boyfriend an hour or so ago. She must have called him to come get her." But before he could say more, Joey began wailing again. Luc sighed. "Can't you stop him? He's been crying like this for the better part of an hour."

"Sorry, but I can't, and walking him isn't going to do it," she said, raising her voice to be heard above the racket. "The only way he'll stop is if Shannon inserts the key in his back or if the battery dies. And the manufacturers make sure those batteries are fairly long-lasting."

Luc groaned and collapsed on the sofa. He massaged his temples and stared down into the face of the crying baby on his lap. "Then we better go find Shannon. My head is about to split wide open."

With no other feasible alternative in sight, Mandy agreed. "Let's go."

Luc scooped up the crying baby, and together, they hurried to Mandy's car. He stopped abruptly at the back bumper and turned to her. "Let's put it in the trunk. That way we won't have to listen to this noise any longer."

"Put him in the trunk?"

Mandy stared at him for a moment in astonishment and then reminded herself they were not dealing with a real infant. Putting the simulator in the trunk would not be a cardinal sin. Besides, she wasn't sure how long Luc had been walking the screaming baby, but, in the short time she'd been listening to Joey's cries, her temples had also begun to throb. She unlocked the trunk, and Luc placed the simulator inside wrapped in a blue receiving blanket and slammed the lid closed. Although the cries could still be heard, they were muffled by the trunk and not nearly as abrasive to their nerves.

Luc leaned against the car and emitted a long sigh. "I find myself almost sympathizing with Shannon. I'm not sure how much more I could have taken of that."

"What if Joey were a real baby? Putting him in the trunk of the car wouldn't have been an option."

He stared at her, mouth agape. "I'm not a Neanderthal. I know that if he were real, this would not be a solution."

She flushed. "I'm sorry. I didn't mean you'd put a real child in a car trunk."

"Absolutely not. I'd have found a way to comfort him and stop his cries. I'm sure that would have done the trick."

Mandy laughed at his optimism. Luc evidently hadn't had much experience with real babies. She tossed him the keys and walked to the passenger's door. "Don't count on it."

An hour later, they had checked the school

where the fall dance was being held, the football field, the outlook on Hawks Mountain where the teens went to park and neck, and Terri's Tearoom where they often congregated after a game or a dance, all to no avail. Shannon and Jeb were nowhere to be found, and Joey was still wailing away in the trunk. In desperation, they decided to head for Jeb Tanner's house, in hopes that perhaps his parents would know where their son and Shannon had gone.

As they made their way through the back roads to the Tanner farm, Mandy turned to Luc. "You were pretty impressive back there with Joey."

He glanced at her. Was she being serious or taunting him? "No caveman attributes?"

The dashboard lights illuminated her face, and her expression looked sincere. "On the contrary, you did everything I've seen a real father do. I think you're a natural candidate for fatherhood."

Her statement stunned him. He'd never thought of himself as a father. Never had any desire to be a father. However, that she thought he'd make a good one warmed him from head to toe. "Thanks."

Silence enveloped the interior of the car. Finally, Mandy turned in her seat to face him. For a moment she said nothing. Luc waited, apprehension growing like a huge fiery ball in his gut. He knew she wanted to say something, but what?

"What did you mean when you told Joey that it's not just single moms who don't want their babies?"

Luc went numb, barely able to feel the steering wheel clutched tightly in his fingers. He'd known for some time that he would eventually have to tell Mandy about his arrangement with Asa and about his childhood in order to make her understand why he'd made the deal. He just hadn't planned on it being so soon.

She placed her hand on his arm. "Luc, please, talk to me."

He glanced at her, trying to read her expression in the lights from the dashboard, but he could only see shadows accentuating the hills and valleys of her features. Was she giving him encouragement or pity? He hoped it wasn't pity because that was the very last thing he wanted from Amantha James.

What do you want from her?

He tried to ignore the taunting voice of his libido. It didn't make any difference what he wanted. It wasn't gonna happen. When he told her about the deal he'd made with a devil named Asa Watkins, he'd have

205

to admit that he came into this whole thing ready to betray her to save his home and his job. She'd hate him, and he'd lose any hope he had of ever starting a relationship with her.

A sharp pain wrapped around his heart. Why should that thought hurt so much when he'd only known her for such a short length of time? Unless. . . . No. It couldn't be. But it sure felt like it.

He'd fallen in love with Mandy.

The thought jarred him so completely that the car swerved into the left lane, right into the path of an oncoming vehicle. Mandy cried out. He quickly jerked the wheel back and managed to get into his own lane before anything catastrophic happened.

He glanced in the rearview mirror and saw the car do a U-turn and come up behind them very quickly. Then bright red and blue lights flashed in the mirror, and the sound of a siren filled the air.

"Terrific," Luc said and pulled the car to the roadside. "Just what we need."

Mandy looked out the back window, then at Luc. "What's he pulling us over for?"

"Because of the way I just swerved, he probably thinks I'm drunk or something. Or it could be because I almost hit him head-on." While they waited for the officer

206

to approach their car, Luc extracted his wallet from his back pocket and slipped his driver's license from inside it.

He looked in the mirror again and groaned. "Crap!"

"What?"

"It's Graylin Talbot, Laureene Talbot's husband. The only way we can get out of this is to fully explain what we're doing. He'll go home and tell Laureene, and this will be all over Carson by morning, along with what the school board is allowing us to do."

Mandy sighed. "I thought we'd dodged the bullet when there was no backlash from Shannon's friends seeing us. But there's no way we won't be exposed now."

They both stared silently out the windshield while they waited for Graylin.

A face appeared outside Luc's window. He rolled it down. "Evenin', Graylin."

The deputy touched the brim of his hat and leaned down to see who was in the passenger's seat. "Evenin', Luc. Miss James." He looked back at Luc. "Drivin' a little careless back there, weren't you, Luc?"

Luc forced a smile. "I was temporarily distracted."

Graylin smiled at Mandy. "I can see as how that might happen." He straightened and backed away from the car. "Suppose you get out of the car and walk the white line for me so I can see it's not more than that."

Luc laid his wallet on the console and climbed from the car. Just then, Joey, who'd been in one of his pre-programmed rest modes, started to wail. Graylin stepped up to the car and glanced in the backseat. Seeing nothing, he turned to Luc, a frown drawing his bushy brows together.

"Where's the baby?"

Luc's stomach hit rock bottom. He sighed. "In the trunk."

Graylin cursed under his breath and threw Luc a contemptuous look. "Open the trunk."

Mandy jumped from the car. "Now, Graylin, we don't want you to get the wrong idea. That's just a —"

Graylin moved a step back, his hand resting on the grip of the pistol strapped to his side. "Miss Mandy, stay right there. Luc, open the trunk." Joey let out another ear-piercing cry. "Now!"

Luc moved slowly to the back of the car, inserted the key and lifted the trunk lid, wishing Joey looked more like a doll and less like a real infant.

Joey lay half under the spare tire, evidently

tossed there when Luc swerved to avoid hitting Deputy Talbot's patrol car.

Cautiously, Graylin stepped forward and peered into the trunk. His eyes bulged, and his mouth fell open. "Good Lord!"

Joey emitted an odd gurgling sound and then went silent.

Mandy sighed. "Thank God, it's dead."

Chapter 13

Graylin stared open-mouthed at Mandy. "Dead? That baby's dead? And you're sayin' that's good?"

"You don't understand." Luc took a step toward the deputy.

The deputy immediately stepped back, his hand still resting on the butt of the gun strapped to his side. He threw a don't-try-anything-stupid look at Luc. "I understand you got a dead baby in your trunk. That's what I understand."

Mandy chimed in. "But it's not a real baby."

Graylin glanced at the simulator and then quickly back to Luc and Mandy. "Looks plenty real to me."

"Well, it's not. It's a simulator." Luc hoped the desperation in his voice didn't make them look worse than the deputy already believed them to be.

Graylin removed his hat and scratched the

top of his head, all the time staring into the trunk. "A simu what?"

"If you just let us explain," Luc pleaded, eager to get back to their search for Shannon.

"Oh, you bet your life you're gonna explain . . . back at the sheriff's office. Git that baby outta the trunk."

Luc's stomach dropped, but he did as Graylin instructed and pulled the simulator from the trunk. Going back to the sheriff's office would waste time, time they needed to be searching for Shannon. "But —"

"No buts about it." Graylin scratched his head, then motioned toward the front of the car. "Now, git in the car and follow me. I never heard of no simul . . . whatever, and that baby looks mighty real to me, so we're going back to the office and sort this out. And don't try anything funny. You wouldn't get to the county line."

Graylin watched closely as Luc took Mandy's arm and walked her to the passenger side of the car. "He's obviously not going to listen to us. But once we get to the sheriff's office, I'll have him call Catherine, and she can explain everything."

Mandy looked at Luc, her worried features illuminated by the full moon. "What about Shannon?"

Luc just shook his head. He wanted to tell her that Shannon would be fine, but he couldn't find the words to express something he had reservations about himself. "There's nothing we can do about her at the moment. We just have to pray that she keeps a solid head on her shoulders and doesn't do anything she'll regret come morning."

Luc and Mandy sat in silence, neither of them able to believe where they were and what had happened. The Carson Sheriff's office was quiet this late at night. Then again, so was the entire town. Granny Jo liked to say they rolled up the streets at nine. Only Jimmy Logan, the town drunk, slouched fast asleep in one of the other cracked vinyl chairs in the holding area. His loud snores reverberated off the colorless walls.

Luc, like everyone else in town, knew the routine. Jimmy would be issued a DUI ticket and spend the night in jail. Tomorrow, sober and ready to start anew, he'd head straight for Route 17 and Hannigan's Bar for his morning eye-opener. Then, after a day of soaking up more booze, the whole process would repeat itself. Luc figured Jimmy had enough tickets to paper his bathroom and then some. Once a year they'd haul him into court; he'd pay his fines and begin a new collection that very day.

Impatient to be out of the stuffy sheriff's office and to find Shannon, Luc glanced at the clock above the desk where a deputy shuffled papers and tried to look busy. Ten twenty-two. Behind him, Deputy Talbot held a phone to his ear, listening intently and occasionally nodding as if the person on the other end could see him. Joey, wrapped in the blue blanket in which they'd placed him in the trunk, lay silent on the desk in front of Graylin.

Luc assumed the person Graylin was talking to was Catherine Daniels. When they'd arrived at the sheriff's office, they'd tried again to explain what was happening, what the simulator was and who they'd been looking for. Graylin hadn't seemed convinced and suspected that something more sinister had been going on. Luc had reluctantly suggested he call Catherine to verify what they'd said. Catherine was not going to be happy that her granddaughter had disappeared, and Luc was not looking forward to having to explain why it happened.

Mandy leaned close to Luc. "Don't look so worried. I'm sure that once he speaks

213

with Catherine, it'll be all straightened out."

Luc leaned closer. For a moment, her perfume wiped all thought from his mind. He straightened away from her and took a deep, cleansing breath to clear his head. "I'm not worried about Graylin. Catherine's explanation may get us off the hook with him, but we'll still have to face her." Luc sighed. "But what worries me more than explaining this mess to Catherine is locating Shannon. Of course, when Graylin goes home, he'll give his darling wife an earful, and by morning Laureene's version of what happened tonight and what's going on at the lake house will be all over town."

Mandy nodded. "Probably. But that's a moot point at this stage, and there's not much we can do about it. What's done is done. And you're right. We need to get out of here and find Shannon. Joey may have stopped crying, but we're still in charge of Shannon."

Luc just hoped they could find her before she did something stupid. She was so determined to hang on to Jeb that it bordered on desperation, and that was not a good sign in a lovesick teenager who wasn't thinking straight.

They both fell silent again.

Just then, Graylin motioned for Mandy to

join him. Slowly, apprehension and dread riding heavy on her shoulders, she got up and walked over to the deputy. He held the phone out to her. "Mrs. Daniels wants to speak to you."

Mandy swallowed hard and took the phone. "Hello, Catherine."

"Mandy, where's Shannon?"

Good question. "She's probably back at the house by now." Mandy hoped Catherine would settle for that explanation, but deep inside, she knew it would take more.

"Probably? That's not good enough. Don't you know?" The panic in Catherine's voice was evident.

"Catherine, you have to understand. Shannon took off without permission. Luc and I have been frantic looking for her." Now she sounded like the one in a panic. She took a deep breath. "We've looked everywhere, and the only possible place she can be is back at the house."

"Graylin is going to release both of you. I'll meet you at the lake house." The line went dead.

Mandy hung up and went back to where Luc waited. She sat down and sighed. "Catherine is not happy. She's going to meet us at the house."

"Did you explain that Shannon just left?"

215

Mandy nodded. "It didn't help. She's understandably scared for her granddaughter. Once we get home and can talk to her, she'll calm down. Hopefully, Shannon will be there, and she can do the explaining."

Luc wiped his hand over his face and shook his head. "If Shannon did anything stupid, like decide to go ahead with her plan to have a baby, we're gonna be the ones explaining."

Mandy didn't want to even think about that. Instead she directed her thoughts to why Shannon had run. Had she been to blame for the girl taking off? Had she pushed her too hard? In her blind-sided attempt to prove her point, had she made her do too much? For the first time ever, Mandy truly understood how difficult dealing with a teenager could be when their hormones were raging and their thinking was clouded by a first love.

Stop beating yourself up! You didn't do any more than you had to to make her see how her life would change with a baby to care for.

Mandy shook her head to dislodge her troublesome thoughts, then picked up the simulator and laid him in her lap. On top of everything else she had to think about tonight, Mandy didn't need to be bombarded by guilt. As she wrapped the blanket

216

around baby Joey, she recalled something Luc had said earlier to the simulator, something Mandy had asked him about, but he had skirted the subject.

She turned on the hard seat to face him, then lowered her voice so no one in the sheriff's office could hear her. "You never answered me."

Mandy's question came out of nowhere. Confused, Luc turned to her. "About what?"

"What you said to Joey about single mommies not being the only ones who don't want their babies."

He'd hoped she'd forgotten about that, but obviously she hadn't, and he could see no way past explaining it to her. Still feeling that in comparison to her childhood, he'd really had it good and had no room to whine, he took a deep breath and began.

"I guess I was drawing on personal experience. My mother was one of those women who never should have been a parent. She told me more times than I can remember that she wished she'd never had me, and that I was just an encumbrance. I don't know why she didn't like me." He paused again, considering what the reason could have been. But just as it had a million times before, the answer eluded him. He stared at the floor, not wanting to see the pity he felt sure he'd see in Mandy's eyes.

"Maybe it wasn't me at all. Maybe it was because her whole life was just a series of disappointments. Not having the career as a dancer that she'd always dreamed of. Not having the man she'd married around to help her raise a little boy." He sighed and shook his head. Now that he's begun verbalizing all the pain and frustration of his childhood, he couldn't seem to stop.

"Maybe my mom was just incapable of really loving anyone. If she did ever love my dad, I think that somewhere along the line she stopped. She treated Dad like dirt. Always arguing with him, telling him she should have married her high school sweetheart. Finding any excuse she could to be away from both of us as much as possible. Most of the time he did a good job of covering up his hurt, but sometimes I could see the disappointment in his face. His family and his marriage had started to crumble around his feet, and he couldn't find a way to stop it. Eventually, it hardened him. It's no wonder his favorite saying was *nothing lasts forever.*" He took a deep breath. "But their rocky marriage wasn't all that unusual. As a child, I saw military families falling apart all around me. Some of them weren't strong enough to withstand the long separations, and some were just not strong, period.

"My father told me once when I was older that two things killed his marriage, the military and love. I decided back then that I'd think long and hard before I fell in love or entered into wedded bliss. I've even considered the possibility that neither was in the cards for me at all."

Mandy's heart ached for the man whose voice echoed with the pain of a neglected child. She knew that pain all too well. Oddly, their childhood circumstances had been polar opposites, but with the same underlying problem . . . a child who had been deprived of the love of a parent. But his last declaration about his views on marriage pierced her right through the heart.

Shoving the deep disappointment aside, Mandy listened intently as Luc began talking again.

"Of course, it didn't help their marriage or me that my dad was too busy working toward making general before he retired, and we moved around a lot. I hated making new friends and entering new schools. Whenever I'd complain, he'd say, 'Nothing lasts forever, boy. Buck up, and make your own way in the world. We all make our own happiness. You don't need to depend on anyone else to do that.' He never understood how much I wanted friends, and how much I wanted to stay where we were and not move again and start all over in a new school. How much I wanted my parents to care about me, to love me." He paused for a thoughtful moment. "Maybe they did. I don't know. All I do know is that they never showed it.

"When I got this job and bought my house, I couldn't believe that I was finally going to put down roots and make friends I could cherish for the rest of my life." He paused. When he spoke again, incredible pain laced through his voice. "And now, that may all be. . . ." He lowered his head and stopped talking.

She touched his forearm. "May all be what?"

"Gone."

"I don't —"

"Okay, folks. Mrs. Daniels verified your story." Deputy Talbot sauntered toward them, thumbs hooked in his belt, with all the attributes of a real life Barney Fife. Mandy had to wonder if the deputy was allowed more than one bullet for the gun strapped to his side. She certainly hoped not. "You can go, but mind you, be careful out there. It's a jungle."

Mandy managed to hold back the laughter until she reached the car. Once out of Deputy Talbot's earshot, both she and Luc collapsed in laughter against the car's fender. Whether from actual amusement or sheer relief, she wasn't sure. But it felt good to release some of the tension that had gripped her body all night.

When she finally got herself under control and looked at Luc, his grin was the first she'd seen from him all night. As usual, her knees threatened to give way, and her heart beat increased threefold.

But even this momentary injection of humor into their evening hadn't made her forget Luc's last words before Talbot interrupted. What had he meant by *gone*? One thing she did understand from what he'd said was that his views on marriage were pretty discouraging. In fact, it sounded to her like the words *relationship* and *commitment* had no place in Luc's vocabulary. If that were the case, then Mandy told herself that she had no business allowing herself to fall in love with him.

But the admonition came much too late. The damage was already done. Amantha James was head over heels in love with Lucas Michaels. Now, she had to figure out what to do about it.

■ ■ ■ ■

After they left the police station, Luc and Mandy, clinging to the hope that Shannon had returned in their absence, headed back to the lake house to meet Catherine. After retrieving Joey from the back seat of the car, they went inside. Though some of the lights were on, a thorough search of the house dashed their hopes of finding Shannon waiting for them.

Mandy put Joey in Shannon's room, then came back downstairs and collapsed on the den couch and buried her face in her hands. She could see all hope of her succeeding at getting the simulators into the school drying up like the morning mist over the lake after the sun came out. If she couldn't keep track of one teenager, what did that do to her credibility?

The couch gave beside her, and she immediately felt the warmth of Luc's thigh pressing against hers. Needing his reassuring presence, she leaned into the warmth of his body. His arm encircled her shoulders, and she sagged against him, taking comfort in his strength and nearness.

"We'll find her. Even if I have to go out and comb every inch of Hawks Mountain and the valley." He spoke with his lips against her hair. "I promise."

She raised her face to look at him. "But what if we can't find her? What if she does something stupid? How will I ever explain to Catherine that I was instrumental in ruining her granddaughter's life?" Her voice caught on a sob.

"You haven't ruined anything, and until we talk to Shannon, we don't know what happened tonight. So stop jumping to conclusions." Luc pressed her head back against his shoulder and tightened his embrace. As usual, Mandy was thinking of the girl and not the effect this would have on her project. "We'll find her before anything like that happens." He hooked his finger under chin and lifted her face up their gazes met.

He started to tell her to go wash her face before Catherine arrived, but the words deserted him. All he could see was the pain in her face and the fear in her eyes. All he could feel was the overwhelming urge to comfort her, to erase the fear. Slowly, he lowered his mouth to hers.

The touch was feather-light. She tasted of salty tears. A soft moan escaped from her as she pressed her lips more firmly against his. Luc battled to hold on to his good sense.

He wanted to scoop her into his arms and carry her upstairs, to hold her through the night, to protect her from anything and everything.

She snuggled closer. His instincts told him to deepen the kiss, but his good sense told him this was neither the time nor the place. Mandy was looking for a shoulder to cry on, nothing more. First and foremost, they had to find Shannon, but after that —

"Geeze. Get a room."

Mandy and Luc sprang apart as if they'd just been caught making out behind the bleachers. They turned toward the voice to find Shannon standing in the doorway, her clothes wrinkled, her hair in disarray and the faint telltale pink of a night of intense necking still evident around her mouth.

Luc jumped to his feet and advanced on the girl. "Where have you been? Joey's been crying, and we've search the whole town for you." Good Lord, he sounded like an irate father, but it didn't stop him. "I think you owe us an explanation."

Shannon pursed her lips and frowned. "I don't have to give any explanations to you. You're not my mother and father." She swung around and hurried toward the stairs. When she reached the bottom stair, she stopped and whirled toward them. "And just in case you're wondering, nothing like you're thinking happened between Jeb and me."

Luc started after her, determined to get answers to where the girl had been and exactly what *nothing happened* meant. She owed Mandy and him that much after all she'd put them through that night. But a hand on his arm stopped him.

"Let her go. We're all upset, and with all our nerves on edge, this could turn into nothing more than a shouting match, and nothing would get accomplished. When Catherine gets here, I'll ask her to wait to talk to Shannon in the morning after we've all had a good night's rest and a chance to calm down. I'm just relieved that she's back." She walked back toward the den, paused and then glanced back at Luc. "I'm beginning to think this whole experiment was a lousy idea."

CHAPTER 14

Luc wasn't sure which tore at his heart more, the defeat coloring Mandy's voice or the way her shoulders sagged. He knew how much succeeding at this meant to her, and if he had the final say, she'd get the simulators into the school. Unfortunately, he didn't have that power, and the people who did might well look upon tonight as an excuse to deny Mandy's request. However, there was something he could do and that was to tell her about the deal that he and Asa had entered into.

Silently, he followed her into the den and guided her toward the big leather sofa. "While we wait for Catherine there's something I need to talk to you about."

She stared up at him. Exhaustion dimmed her eyes. It had been a long, frustrating night, and he hated to add to it, but he was determined this time to come clean and clear the air between them once and for all.

"Can't this wait until morning?"

He shook his head. "No, it's waited too long already."

Luc joined Mandy on the sofa, but before he could figure out where to start, the sound of the front door opening and closing told him that once more fate was not in his corner. Any explanation would have to wait.

Seconds later, an unusually disheveled Catherine Daniels rushed into the room. "Where's my granddaughter?"

Luc jumped to his feet. "She's upstairs. She got home minutes after we did."

Catherine looked from him to Mandy, her expression anxious. "Is she all right?"

Luc took her arm and led her to the chair opposite them. He waited until she'd seated herself and returned to his seat beside Mandy. "She's gone to bed, and she's fine. Defiant, but fine."

"Where was she? Did she tell you?"

How Luc would have loved to just bypass that question. But he couldn't. Catherine deserved an answer.

From the corner of his eyes, he saw Mandy glance at him, then she met Catherine's inquisition eye-to-eye. "She was with Jeb. Other than that we don't know anything." Quickly, she followed up with, "Everyone's really tired, so Luc and I felt it

227

better to wait until tomorrow, after we've all rested and calmed down, before we started questioning her." Mandy shifted her position on the couch and folded her hands in her lap.

"I . . . I've been thinking." Mandy glanced at Luc, then back to Catherine. "I think we should call this whole thing off. It was a bad idea from the start."

Although stunned by her announcement, Luc's main concern then was Mandy, so he kept his gaze centered on her. She looked so fragile. Like the merest touch would shatter her into tiny pieces. He wanted to hold her, protect her and tell her everything would be okay, but he was afraid that once he held her, he'd never let her go, and there was still so much between them that had to be cleared up.

He glanced at Catherine. Her anxious expression had turned to cold anger, and strangely enough, it was directed at him. Why was she so mad at him? Was it because they'd lost track of Shannon, and her grandmother held him accountable? Was it because they hadn't found out where she'd been all that time? Or was it —

Suddenly, a bad feeling began forming in the pit of his stomach.

"Well, this must make you happy, Luc,"

Catherine said, her voice as cold and crisp as her expression.

Still at a loss for this change in the woman, Luc frowned. "I don't —"

Catherine stood and walked toward Luc, her hand on her hip, her posture rigid, her gaze accusing. "Don't act like you don't know what I'm talking about. I had a long talk with Asa Watkins today, and he told me all about the little deal you two had."

Mandy frowned, her head turning first to Catherine then Luc. "Deal? What kind of deal? What's she talking about, Luc?"

Luc couldn't speak, couldn't look at Mandy. Couldn't stand to see what she could only interpret as his treachery mirrored in her eyes. After a few moments, he chanced a glance at her. She stared back at him, open-mouthed, her beautiful coffee-colored eyes filled with distrust.

If Catherine had only been a few minutes later arriving, he'd have been able to break this to Mandy slowly and help her understand that he'd changed his mind, and that introducing the simulators into the school held immense merit. But now, the horse was out of the barn, and he was left to explain why to a woman who looked like he had just stabbed her through the heart.

Finally, when he had offered no explanation, Mandy turned back to Catherine. "What deal?"

Catherine threw one last glare in Luc's direction and then met Mandy's questioning expression head-on. "It seems that Luc was supposed to make sure from the get-go that this experiment of ours failed. If Luc made sure that happened, Asa would win his bid to keep the simulators out of the school, and as a result, maintain his athletic budget. The payoff was a guarantee that Luc's contract would be renewed by the school board." She stiffened her back and glared at Luc. "Congratulations, Luc." Then she turned back to Mandy. "I'm assuming that our experiment is over, so I'll be by in the morning to pick up Shannon and take her home." Then, without another word, she left.

Mandy waited for Luc to say something, but he didn't. "You have nothing to say?"

He looked at her and shook his head. "Would you believe me if I did?"

"Since you've been lying to me all this time, no, I probably wouldn't."

Mandy stood and without looking at him, left the den and climbed the stairs to her room. Once there, she closed the door and sagged against its solid surface as the tears began to slide down her cheeks. Tears she'd been struggling to hold back ever since she realized that Luc had betrayed her.

How could he do this to her? He knew how important it was to her. He'd given her the impression that he was just as eager to protect the kids as she was. It had all been a lie. Even the kiss and his supposed understanding when she'd poured out the story of her childhood. All lies. What a gullible fool she'd been. All the time he'd been charming her so she wouldn't suspect he was scheming with Asa to make sure she failed.

She dried her tears and pushed away from the door. Her mother had been right. Men couldn't be trusted. They lie and trample over your heart. Mandy hauled her suitcase from the closet and began throwing clothes into it. She'd leave here as soon as she'd settled things with Shannon.

If her attitude tonight was anything to go by, the teen was ready to throw in the towel. Under any other circumstances, Mandy would have been celebrating her victory. But all she could feel was the pain of Luc's betrayal gripping her heart in an iron fist. All she wanted now was to get out of this house and as far away from Luc as possible.

The next morning, Shannon flounced into

the kitchen sporting major attitude and carrying Joey by one arm. Mandy hadn't had a chance to change Joey's batteries, so he was not reacting to the rough treatment. The teen flopped the simulator on the table in front of Mandy.

Mandy fingered it and looked at the teenager. "What's this mean?" She already knew that it meant Shannon's surrender, but Mandy wanted to hear it from her.

"Luc was right."

Mandy stiffened and set her coffee cup on the table. A ball of dread the size of Hawks Mountain settled in her stomach. She wasn't sure she was ready to hear any more of Luc's betrayals. Nevertheless, she forced herself to ask. "Right about what?"

"He said I should be out having fun with my friends."

"That's not what I said." Luc entered the kitchen, his face contorted in a scowl. "I said I understood your frustration, and that you'd rather be out having fun with your friends, but that you should stick it out."

And if Shannon stuck it out, Mandy would lose her bid to get the simulators into the school. The anger she'd experienced last night returned. "And if she stuck it out, you and Asa would win. Right?"

Shannon's gaze bounced from Mandy to

Luc. "Mr. Watkins? Win what? What's he got to do with this?"

Luc ignored the question and ran his fingers through his hair. "No. That's not why I wanted her to stick it out."

Mandy lunged to her feet, her hands fisted at her sides. "Why then?" Last night she'd vowed not to get into a fight with Luc about this, but her anger and the intense pain of his betrayal had gotten the best of her.

"Are you going to listen if I try to explain?" Luc's voice had gained in volume.

"Are you going to tell me the truth?" Mandy's tone matched his.

"I'm not going to tell you anything if you're going to listen with a closed mind."

They glared at each other. Luc opened his mouth to say something else, but Shannon's shrill cry stopped him.

"Stop it!" She stomped her foot. "Stop yelling at each other. You sound like my parents. You win. Okay? My parents win. I don't want to have a baby anymore." Her tone of voice told of the tears she was fighting to hold back. "It's over. Done. I'm going home. My grandmother's coming to pick me up." She turned and fled the kitchen.

After Mandy had slipped from the lake

house, she had driven blindly, barely aware of maneuvering the car over the curving mountain roads. Though her anger at Luc had flared brightly in the kitchen, once away from the house, all that was left of it were the ashes of a dream that she'd foolishly allowed herself to believe could come true.

How could she have fallen into the very trap she'd so carefully avoided for years? Though she'd dated, she'd made certain that her heart had never become involved. The one time she'd lowered her guard and let a man slip by her defenses, she'd ended up paying the price. The one good thing that had come out of it was that she hadn't been really stupid and fallen into bed with him and ended up like her mother, single and raising a baby on her own. Not that she wouldn't have loved it and devoted herself to it. It was just that babies needed fathers and a mother who had time to love it and care for it. She could only offer the love and care.

Mandy was about certain that the simulators would be introduced into the school. It had come down to putting the experiment's success before the school board and getting their vote. But the victory was hollow. In winning one battle, she'd lost Luc and any hope of a future with him.

Mandy rounded a curve in the road and stopped the car. She shifted it to *park* and looked around, dazed and confused as to why she had chosen to come here. Why was she in front of this large white farm house . . . Granny Jo Hawks' house?

Before she could shift the car into drive and leave, Granny Jo's big, gray dog, Jake, sprang to his feet and began barking, announcing her arrival. Seconds later, the front door opened, and Granny Jo stepped onto the porch, a big smile creasing her kindly face. At that moment, Mandy realized why she'd come here. Becky had told Mandy if she ever had a problem, there was no one better at sorting than her grandmother.

"Well, child, are you going to sit there all day, or are you coming inside?" Granny called.

Mandy couldn't very well drive away now. She turned off the engine. "Only if you have the coffee pot on," she called back, trying to inject the happiness she didn't feel into her voice.

"Well, if I don't, I can soon fix that."

Mandy climbed from the car, walked up the rose bush-lined front walk and was immediately enveloped in the warmth of Granny Jo's loving embrace. Tears welled up in Mandy's eyes.

"This is a nice surprise," Granny said over Mandy's shoulder, then held her at arm's length and gazed deep into her eyes. A frown wrinkled her brow. "Now, now. Nothing's that bad." She used the corner of her apron to dry Mandy's eyes and then wrapped her arm around her. "I just took a batch of sugar cookies out of the oven. How about we have us one or two and a hot cup of coffee and we'll see if we can sort out whatever it is that has you upset. My Earl used to say that my sugar cookies could cure anything."

Granny's caring and love swamped Mandy's emotions. She nodded, unable to speak for fear the tears once again threatening to fall would be let loose.

Moments later, they were seated at Granny Jo's kitchen table. The aroma of fresh baked cookies filled the room. Mandy inhaled deeply. Unbelievably, this was the first time in her life she'd ever smelled freshly baked anything. To her, it was like smelling the most expensive Paris perfume. Surely this was what a home should smell like . . . like love and comfort and all the things she'd never had as a child. And that's how she suddenly felt . . . like a child. A child seeking comfort, love . . . and advice.

CHAPTER 15

Granny Jo poured coffee for each of them. Then she set a pitcher of cream, a bowl of sugar and a plate of golden brown cookies on the table. The sunlight coming through the kitchen window bounced off the sugar crystals atop the cookies, turning them to jewel encrusted confections.

Mandy stared transfixed at the plate, her thoughts swirling as she searched for an explanation as to why she'd ended up on Granny Jo's doorstep. Instinct maybe. Many times at the office Mandy had listened to Granny offer Becky her homespun advice. Perhaps her subconscious knew that Granny may have some answers for her, too.

Granny Jo chuckled and pointed toward the untouched treat. "You're supposed to eat them, child, not admire them."

Mandy roused herself, smiled and took a cookie. She bit into it. The sweet goodness exploded on her tongue. The only cookies she'd ever eaten had been mass-produced and packaged in cardboard boxes. And those occasions had been rare. These tasted like a slice of pure heaven. Maybe Mr. Hawks had been right. Maybe Granny Jo's cookies could cure anything.

The thought had no sooner passed through her mind than the pain returned. She wasn't sure a panacea existed that could erase the hurt that Luc had inflicted with his lies.

Mandy's pleasure in the sweet treat vanished. She set it unfinished on her plate.

"If my baking can't keep a smile on your pretty face, then this must be serious." Granny Jo covered Mandy's hand with her own and squeezed gently. "What is it, dear?"

Unexpected tears welled up in Mandy's eyes so fast she didn't have time to wipe them away before they overflowed down her cheeks. The next thing she knew, sobs tore from her in great, rasping gasps.

Granny Jo hiked her chair around the table to get closer to Mandy and drew her into her arms and cradled her head against her ample bosom. "My word, child, you're breaking my heart." She laid her cheek against the top of Mandy's head. As Mandy's sobs subsided, Granny Jo drew a handkerchief from her apron pocket and pressed it into Mandy's hand. "Suppose you dry those tears and then tell me what's got you in this state, and we'll see if we can sort it out."

Mandy swallowed, wiped at her cheeks with the handkerchief, blew her nose and took a deep breath in an effort to get a hold on her out-of-control emotions.

Finally, she choked out, "Luc."

Granny Jo nodded sagely. "I might have known there was a man at the bottom of this." She moved back to her side of the table, folded her hands on the placemat and sighed. "Tell me what he's done to upset you so much."

Mandy took a sip of her coffee and spilled the entire story, leaving out nothing. "He acted like he was supporting me, Granny Jo, but all the time he was plotting behind my back with Asa to see me fail."

Granny sat back in her chair. "I'm surprised that Catherine had any part in this, but I can understand her need to help Shannon. What doesn't surprise me is that Asa Watkins stuck his nose in and gummed up the works. My Earl loved his ball games, but that man has an addiction to athletics that just isn't healthy. He never could see that a good education was better than being able to throw a football."

She got up and refilled their coffee cups. "Might as well leave this here," she said, setting the coffee pot on a hot plate next to the sugar and creamer. "Looks like we're gonna be here for a spell."

Mandy forced a half smile, but she felt it crumble as quickly as it appeared. "So what do I do about Luc?"

"You know, Mandy, things are not always like they seem."

"I don't understand."

"First of all, are you sure he actually lied to you? And are you sure it's the lie that is bothering you, or the damage to your heart?"

A silence fell over the room as Mandy gave Granny's question serious thought. She had no need to even consider the last part of Granny's question. She knew the answer. The damage to her heart was something that would probably lay raw for some time to come. She'd given Luc a gift she'd never given to another person . . . her trust. And he'd violated it.

But that was over and done, and although her heart ached, there wasn't anything she could do about it. Right now she needed to concentrate on the students and what this meant for them. So, that left her back at Granny's first question. Had Luc actually lied? Not actually. But he'd led her to believe otherwise.

"Luc lied by omission. He never voiced the actual lie, but he never told me what he was doing either. He let me believe he was supporting me."

To Mandy's surprise, Granny Jo laughed. "Child, I've learned over the years that men and women have totally different ideas of what's right and what's wrong. God love them, men have a notion that they're not lying if they don't tell us everything."

"What do you mean they think they're not lying? That doesn't make sense. Of course they're lying."

For a while, Granny Jo said nothing. Finally, after a couple of sips of coffee, she set aside her cup and leaned her forearms on the table.

"Back when Earl and I had only been married a few years, Bill Keeler's son came down with mono and couldn't go to the produce market in Charleston to help his father. Because Earl and Bill were friends, Earl volunteered to go with him instead. I knew that Bill was fond of his whiskey, and the trip would inevitably end up with a night of drinking, so I made Earl promise not to drink and not to let Bill drive home. That evening, after they'd picked up the produce, as I suspected they would, they went out for a few drinks."

Granny topped off the coffee for both of them.

As she added more sugar and cream to her cup, Mandy wondered where this story was going.

"Long about two in the morning, I got a call to come bail my husband out of the Charleston County jail." Mandy gasped. "I can tell you, I was not at all happy with Earl Hawks. I didn't talk to him all the way home and for another week after that.

"He tried to explain. Said it was just a disagreement between him and another fella in the bar. I didn't believe it." Granny picked at a loose thread in the placemat and began wrapping it around her index finger. "My Earl was a peace-loving, Christian man who would have walked away before he settled anything with violence. I knew it would have taken a lot to get him to double up his fists and hit a man. So, I also knew he was leaving something out. Something he wasn't telling me. And of course, the more I thought about it, the madder I got."

Mandy leaned forward, eager to hear more, but still unsure why Granny was telling this story. Fighting not to show her impatience, she gripped her hands together

242

in her lap. She'd heard Granny Jo's stories before, and she knew that she'd eventually reach the end, and that often a small seed of wisdom could be found in the lengthy tale. Mandy just had to be patient.

"A few weeks later, I ran into Bill's wife at a church social. We got to talking about one thing and another, and we started comparing notes about that night. It was then that I learned what had happened that started the fight. Turns out the fella in the bar was my elder brother Brandon, the uppity one, Alyce's granddad. Seems Brandon said something about me that got Earl's dander up, and when my brother refused to take it back, Earl hit him. Bill wouldn't tell his missus what my brother said to Earl, and Earl wouldn't say either. Took it to his grave with him. To this day I don't know what started that fight, but I do know Earl was defending my honor, and for that, I was very proud of him. And by not letting on that it was my own brother who started it, he was sparing my feelings." Granny patted Mandy's hand. "So, you see? They have their reasons for skirting the whole story when they don't tell us everything. And sometimes it's for our own good." She winked. "At least they think it's for our own good."

Mandy frowned. "But why would not telling me about his deal with Asa be for my own good?"

"Maybe it wasn't. Maybe it was. Maybe it was because he'd figured you'd have this reaction. Then again, maybe it was because he was afraid of losing you. Truth of it is, you won't know unless you talk it out with him. I'm sure he had good reason not to say anything to you." She squeezed Mandy's hand. "Lucas Michaels is a good man, child. He wouldn't hurt a flea intentionally. My guess is that Asa trapped him somehow between a rock and a hard place, and Luc had no choice."

A loud bark sounded outside the back door. Granny stood and went to let Jake in. The big dog lumbered into the kitchen, stopped to get a quick scratch from his mistress, then flopped down beside the stove and closed his eyes. The older woman watched him for a moment, then came back to the table and rested her hand on Mandy's shoulder. "If you ask me, young lady, I think he hurt your heart more than he violated your trust."

Luc stared blankly out the window of his house. The place he'd always treasured as his haven suddenly felt alien and empty to him. He turned from the window and looked around the living room, knowing that he'd soon have to leave here for good. He'd have to say goodbye to the friends he'd made and the town he'd come to love.

All the old resentments and pain he'd known every time his father had been reassigned and they'd had to move, came back to sit on his chest like a lead weight. He took a deep breath in an effort to dispel the feeling, but the heaviness remained.

"It's your own fault," he told himself. "You're the one who let Asa corner you into taking part in his scheme. You should have stood up to him and told him to put his deal where the sun don't shine."

If he'd had the guts to stonewall Asa, Luc would still be losing everything he cherished, but at least he'd be leaving Carson with a clear conscience, his dignity intact and the knowledge that he did the right thing for the kids. And just maybe, he wouldn't be losing Mandy.

He flopped down on the sofa. Mandy hated him for deceiving her, and he couldn't blame her. She'd given him something he'd guessed she hadn't given many people — her trust, and he'd betrayed it.

Even though his attempt to make Shannon see what she'd be taking on as a single mother had been sincere, Mandy saw it now as a false front to make her think he was on her side, a way to seal his deal with Asa Watkins. If he told her now that he'd decided long ago not to go along with Asa's plan, she wouldn't believe him. Either way it was a lose/lose situation.

Worst of all, she didn't even believe his sincerity when he'd kissed her or when he'd listened to her story of her miserable childhood. Bottom line was he'd lost her trust and any chance of winning her love.

"You really screwed things up, Michaels."

The ringing phone cut through his thoughts. Luc wasn't in any mood to talk to anyone, so he let the answering machine pick it up.

"Michaels. Asa Watkins here. I hope your résumé is up to date and your bags are packed, because I have a feeling you'll be on the unemployment line after next week's school board meeting. Next Tuesday. Seven o'clock. School library. Be there."

Click.

CHAPTER 16

Seven days later, Luc sat in the front row of folding chairs in the library. He'd contemplated sitting in the back, but decided if he was about to be canned, he'd sit up front and face it with dignity, not hiding in the back of the room. Asa had held him under his thumb for the last time.

He glanced at the clock. Six fifty-five. Five more minutes, and he'd be on the road to unemployment. In the past week, he'd thought about his fate so much that his mind had gone numb, and any effort on his part to sort through his future failed. As his students were fond of saying when faced with what appeared to be a hopeless situation . . . it is what it is.

The one good thing that would come out of this evening was that Mandy would most likely get the simulators into the Family Planning Class.

As he waited, the board table across the

front of the room remained empty, while the rest of the seats in the library slowly began to fill. Normally a school board meeting was scantily attended, but tonight it appeared as though the entire town had turned out. As people filed past him, some smiled, others avoided eye contact. Laureene Talbot looked at him, then tilted her nose to the heavens in disdain, emitted a loud *huff* flavored heavily with disapproval and hurried to the opposite side of the room.

Evidently Graylin had told his wife the whole story of the test and the baby simulators. And she'll probably tell the entire town tonight. Wonderful!

Luc tried very hard not to show his discomfort and greeted everyone who spoke to him as though nothing were any different than any other meeting of the Carson School Board. But it wasn't easy. He wanted to stand up and tell them what a jerk they had running the board, but he didn't.

Even more than that, he wanted to leave before Mandy came in. Having to face her disappointment in him again, and then get public confirmation of his deal with Asa, held about as much appeal as running naked across the town square in the middle of winter.

Then he felt it. That unmistakable tug at his heart whenever Mandy was near. Slowly, he turned to look toward the door. There she was. This time his heart tripled its beat, and the air seemed to leave his lungs.

Like a man dying of thirst, he drank in every inch of her. It had only been a few days since he'd last seen her, but it seemed like months. She was even lovelier than the image he'd stored away in his memory. Her auburn hair lay in soft waves over the shoulders of a hunter green sweater which hugged her breasts and her slim waist. The fluorescent lights caught in the strands of her hair, turning them to a fiery red. As he watched her, she glanced in his direction, disappointment still evident in her expression. But even faced with her disenchanted gaze, he couldn't seem to tear his eyes away from her.

She walked to the row of chairs across the aisle from where Luc sat and took the very last seat on the far end beside Becky Hart and Granny Jo Hawks. Mandy sat all the way back in her chair, folded her hands in her lap and stared straight ahead. With her out of his line of vision, Luc sighed and turned his attention to the five people filing in behind the head table.

Bill Keeler, his flushed cheeks attesting to

a side trip to Hannigan's Bar, led the way. Reverend Thomas, looking solemn in his Sunday clergy clothes, was next in line. Catherine Daniels, serene and stately in her usual custom-tailored gray suit, preceded the board's accountant, Charles Henderson, a short, balding man, who appeared so timid that he'd dissolve into a puddle of nerves if anyone said *boo* to him. Last, but not least, and making his grand entrance, strode a frowning Asa Watkins.

Not one of them met Luc's gaze. He took a deep breath and straightened in his chair. If he'd hoped for a reprieve, that dream vanished instantly. From the collective expressions on the board's faces, his goose had probably been cooked before the doors to the library had opened that night. Resigned to his fate, he leaned back and waited for the axe to fall.

"You okay?"

Granny Jo's whisper roused Mandy from her contemplation of the man seated on the other side of the library. Though she couldn't see him, every nerve in Mandy's body thrummed with awareness of Luc's presence.

"Fine." Mandy smiled to reinforce her lie. She wasn't fine at all. Her nerves felt like the tangled kudzu vines covering the trees on the roadside near the lake. Her hands were as cold as ice.

"I'm sure the board will okay buying the simulators." Becky squeezed her hand reassuringly.

Mandy forced a smile. "I hope you're right." She was certain of Catherine's endorsement, but she had no idea how the other board members would vote. At this point, it was a crap shoot.

Both Becky and Granny had insisted on accompanying her to the meeting for moral support. Though deeply appreciative of their kind gesture and concern, she'd tried to assure them that they didn't have to, and that she would be fine. Neither would hear of her going alone to face what they had categorized by the three of them as "The Inquisition."

Oddly enough, right now, Mandy's thoughts centered less on the board buying the simulators for the school's Family Planning classes, and more on wrestling with how she felt about Luc. She'd thought she was prepared to see him again, but when she'd looked into his worried face, her heart ached for him.

Knowing how much he treasured his home and the roots he'd put down in Carson, she knew if he had to leave because the school board terminated his job, it would be one of the hardest things he'd ever had to do. And, in a way, she felt partially responsible. After all, if she hadn't tried to introduce the simulators into the school, and if she hadn't gone along with Catherine's proposal, none of this would have happened. She should have said no to Catherine and found another way to get the simulators incorporated into the curriculum that didn't involve Luc.

Hindsight's twenty-twenty.

All the *would haves* and *could haves* her conscience might conjure up wouldn't change a thing. Nor would wishing things were different between her and Luc.

She'd thought a lot about what Granny Jo had told her about men not telling the whole truth. Had that been the case with Luc? Had he been trying to protect her from Asa's underhanded manipulations? Ever since she'd left Granny's that day, Mandy had searched her memory for any sign she'd missed that Luc had been undermining her cause. But she could find none. In fact, everything he'd done seemed to support her.

He'd backed her up every time she'd had a confrontation with Shannon. He'd gone out of his way to make sure Alyce got the opportunity to go for her GED. He'd helped Mandy scour the countryside looking for Shannon the night she'd taken off. And worried as much as Mandy had about where the teen was and what she was doing.

Mandy sighed. But even if he hadn't betrayed her or, if as Granny suggested, he'd lied to protect Mandy, there was still the issue that Luc didn't want commitment, didn't want marriage or kids, and Mandy would settle for no less. She would not live the kind of life her mother had, hopping from man to man and lying to herself that one of them loved her enough to stay and make a home. Early on Mandy had sworn that any relationship she got into had to be serious and permanent — forever. Since Luc didn't believe in forever —

"Meeting will come to order." Asa's strident voice and the hollow sound of his gavel hitting the table interrupted her musings. After checking to see that any conversation had ceased, he glanced down at the papers in front of him. "Our first order of business is the new teacher for the tenth grade Geometry class." He slid a paper from a manila folder. "I have a copy of her résumé here."

He read the résumé aloud. The board discussed the pros and cons of hiring this woman and eventually decided to give her the job. The next order of business was approval of new text books for the English class. This entailed discussion of the merits of the author and reading the opinions expressed by the state on the book. After more than an hour of back and forth argument, the board decided against the book being used in the Carson schools.

Mandy fidgeted in her seat. How much longer would she have to sit here and wait? She had a feeling that Asa was intentionally putting off the question of buying the simulators until the last thing on his agenda. Biting her tongue to keep from saying something, she glanced over at Luc. His jaw was set in a straight line. Obviously he realized what Asa was doing as well and was no happier about it than she was.

The meeting droned on, stretching Mandy's nerves to the breaking point.

Finally, Asa announced the next order of business. "The question before the board is whether or not to include those . . . uh. . . ."

"Baby simulators," Catherine offered.

He cleared his throat as if the very thought of verbalizing the name of the artificial babies was distasteful to him. "Yes, those *things* into the Family Planning Class." He turned to Catherine. "How did your experiment work out?"

"I'll tell you how it worked out." Laureene Talbot sprang to her feet as though she'd been sitting on a springboard just waiting for this to come up. Her shoulders were squared, her nose slightly elevated. "Shamelessly, that's how. I cannot believe this board approved of two single people and a young, innocent, teenage girl living alone in an isolated house with no supervision." She addressed her final remarks to the gathering and not the board. She turned back to the five people at the head table. "And you, Reverend Thomas, a man of God and a member of the board, allowing this to go on. I'm appalled." She sniffed indignantly and turned to once more address the town's people. "My husband caught them riding around with one of those . . . *things* in the trunk of the car screaming its lungs out. They'd lost track of the teenager they'd been put in charge of and were out looking for her. It leaves one to wonder exactly what *they* were doing when the girl ran off."

Mandy cringed. She'd worried that this was going to happen, but she hadn't come close to guessing how humiliated she'd feel if it did. Laureene made it sound like the board had been running a brothel, and she and Luc had engaged in orgies every night.

"They lived out there for almost two weeks. Two weeks! They —"

When she could stand it no longer, Mandy jumped to her feet. "It wasn't like that."

"Oh, really? Well, suppose you tell us just what it was like, *Miss James*?" Obviously thinking she'd cornered her prey, Laureene's thin lips curled into a knowing smile.

"I'll tell you what it was like, *Mrs. Talbot*."

All eyes in the room turned to the other side of the library where Luc stood facing the older woman, hands on his hips and with protecting Mandy from the woman's barbs paramount in his heart and mind.

"You tell that old busy body, Luc." Granny Jo's voice cut through the expectant silence, and from the corner of his eye he saw Catherine smile and nod.

"It was like a family. A real family. And none of the dirty little scenarios that have passed through your overly active imagination were part of it." He walked to the center front and glared at Laureene. "It was teaching a young girl the financial, physical and personal hardships of a life as a single mother with a tiny baby to be responsible for." He moved closer to the woman who had flopped back into her seat and cowed as if she'd like to hide beneath it. "Miss James did nothing to be ashamed of, nothing that she couldn't stand before you and relate in full detail. Nothing."

He turned back to the people sitting at the board table. Now that he'd gotten started, Luc was determined to clear the air once and for all.

"I, on the other hand, can't say the same." A *huff* of satisfaction came from the vicinity of Laureene's chair. He ignored her. "I entered into an agreement with this man." He pointed an accusing finger at Asa Watkins. A gasp went up from the gathering. "The understanding was that in exchange for sabotaging Miss James' bid to introduce the baby simulators into the school, Asa would see to it that my contract with the Carson School District would be renewed. It's not something I'm proud of. Until Miss James educated me about the kind of life a single mother had to endure, I had nothing on my mind but to stay in Carson, to keep the home I love in a community I love." He took a deep, cleansing breath, the first he'd been able to take since that day in Asa's office a few weeks ago. "Having seen the hardships firsthand, I can say that it seems to be a very effective way to curb teenage pregnancy. Therefore, I am recommending to

257

the board that they take whatever they need from the athletic fund and buy the baby simulators and incorporate them into the school's curriculum."

Luc turned back to Asa and smiled.

Asa glared at him and mouthed, *You're fired.*

Luc's smile widened. "I quit."

CHAPTER 17

Mandy gazed in stunned silence at the spot where Luc had stood moments ago. For a long time after Luc quit and then walked out of the library, the room held the same shocked silence.

Had she really heard what her brain said she did? Had Luc not only endorsed the purchase of the simulators, but he'd also risen to her defense against Laureene's insinuations? Though she was thankful, and it had warmed her heart beyond description, it somehow made the thought that they could never have a relationship harder to bear. If only —

"How can you people just let Mr. Michaels quit?" The distressed, young female's voice emanated from the rear of the room.

All heads swiveled in her direction.

"Shannon. What are you doing here?" Catherine Daniels had come to her feet and directed all her attention on her granddaughter.

Shannon and a young man Mandy didn't recognize hurried to the front of the room. "Jeb and I came to tell everyone that what Mr. Michaels and Miss James did was a good thing. If I hadn't gone to stay with them, I never would have realized how much of my life would have been ruined by having a baby now." She turned toward the gathered people. "I still want to be a mom one day, but not until I've been a teenager. I want to go to the prom, go to college and get a good education for a future career, maybe even join a sorority. I never would have seen all that without Joey . . . without the simulator." She swung back to the board. "You have to get Mr. Michaels back."

Jeb took Shannon's hand and stood shoulder to shoulder with her. "And Mr. Michaels made me see that my education should be my priority and not sports."

Asa sprang to his feet. "Now, hold on, Jeb. How do you think you'll pay for college without an athletic scholarship?"

Mandy smiled inwardly, knowing Asa was seeing his dream of Carson having nurtured the star quarterback on the UCLA football team go up in smoke.

Jeb shrugged. "If I can't get my grades up high enough to get into the school, what good's an athletic scholarship going to do me? Worse comes to worse, I'll just have to get a job to pay my way, I guess." He faced the room full of people. "Bottom line is Mr. Michaels is the best thing that ever happened to Carson High, and you need to make sure he stays here."

"That's impossible. He just quit." Asa's voice rang out in the room like an executioner's proclamation that the criminal had succumbed, drowning out the shouts of agreement with Jeb's statement. "It's a done deal."

"The only thing that's a done deal in this life, Asa, is death." Granny Jo went to stand with Jeb and Shannon, forming what was quickly becoming an impenetrable human wall of protest in front of a red-faced Asa Watkins. "Luc Michaels made it possible for my granddaughter to get her GED, then go to school to start a career so she can support her baby. And after hearing these young people attest to his help, I'd say his interest lies more in the students than adding any more trophies to that glass case in your office."

Asa sputtered, but couldn't seem to form a coherent reply.

Luc had stood up for her, now Granny Jo and these teens were doing likewise. It was

261

Mandy's turn to support him and these students. She rose to her feet and joined the other three in front of the board table. "You blackmailed an honorable man into trying to undermine the test that Catherine suggested to prove the simulators were a good way to prevent teen pregnancy. But despite the danger of him losing his job, his home and a community he cherishes, he never once did anything to jeopardize the test. Personally, I think anyone who would sink as low as you did has no place on the school board."

"Now, wait just a minute. You can't —" On his feet now, his fists planted on the table, Asa's complexion had gone from blood-vessel-popping red to apoplexy purple.

"No, you wait!" Catherine Daniels, who had reseated herself after the teens began presenting their case, had come to her feet again. Her tone of voice and expression seemed to set Asa back a bit. "This board appointed you, and we can just as quickly unappoint you."

Mandy wanted to burst into applause, but she waited to see where Catherine was going with this, hoping it was in the direction of Asa's termination. Mandy looked at the other board members. Would they defy Asa?

"I say we take a vote right now," Catherine said, her tone decisive and clear. "I make a motion to remove Asa Watkins as Carson's School Superintendent. Do I have a second?"

Throwing a disapproving glance in Asa's direction, Reverend Thomas raised his hand. "I'll second it."

"Discussion?" Catherine asked.

Granny Jo took a step forward. "I think we've about discussed this to death."

"Granny's right." Reverend Thomas, who had remained silent throughout the discussion of Asa's transgressions, spoke with the authoritative voice he usually reserved for Sunday mornings. "No need for any more talk. I think we've all seen the light. Let's vote."

Again, applause broke out from the crowd. Catherine waved her hand to quiet them and turned to the other people sharing the front table with her. "Well?"

All the board members nodded their agreement.

Asa, who had been glaring at Reverend Thomas, transferred his searing gaze to Catherine. "This is most — Most . . . un-Parliamentary. Robert's Rules of —" His puttered protest went unheeded.

"Very well then, let's vote." Catherine cut

him off before he could finish his sentence. "All in favor?"

Mandy held her breath. Would they have enough backbone to go up against the man who'd threatened, bullied and now black-mailed them into thinking his way and kept them cowed with his iron-fisted rule?

The remaining board members looked at each other, as if waiting for one of them to make the first move. Finally Bill Keeler raised his hand. "I'm tired of you telling me what to do, how I should think and where I should go, Asa. I vote yes."

Reverend Thomas and Charles Henderson quickly followed suit. "I vote yes," they chimed simultaneously.

"Opposed?"

Mandy hid a grin behind her hand as Asa's hand shot into the air. Then he looked around at an entire room of accusing eyes directed at him and slowly lowered it.

Catherine grabbed Asa's gavel and struck the table once. "Majority rules. Motion is passed." Then she turned to the ex-superintendent and grinned. "It appears as though your services are no longer needed here, Asa."

A roar of applause went up from the gathering.

Mandy fought once more to suppress her

smile. She just wished Luc could have been here to see this.

Asa huffed loudly. No doubt the sound of the wind leaving his sails. He snatched his gavel from Catherine. "You'll be sorry you did this."

"You might want to be careful about threatening anyone with so many witnesses present, Asa." Catherine motioned toward the gathered townspeople, her lips still curled in a satisfied grin. "You have no sway over this board anymore."

Asa glared at each of the board members in turn and then stalked from the room, his face now a lighter shade of purple, and his precious gavel clutched tightly in his fist.

Catherine retook her seat. Mandy and Granny Jo returned to theirs. Jeb and Shannon found seats in the back of the room.

Catherine folded her arms on the table and looked thoughtful. "Well, this is all well and good, but it seems to leave us with a bit of a dilemma. We now have no superintendent."

A thought occurred to Mandy. Something that made perfect sense. She raised her hand. "I have a suggestion."

Luc had driven around aimlessly for the last hour, still stunned at what he'd done. He hadn't gone to the meeting with the intention of quitting his job. Quite the contrary. He'd been prepared to do whatever was necessary to save it. Then he'd seen Mandy. At that moment, he knew he could do no less than to admit what he and Asa had done and expose Asa for the manipulative, underhanded control freak that he was.

And when Laureene started casting aspersions on Mandy, he could not sit there and listen to the woman he loved being slandered. Mandy had done nothing to deserve that. When she'd entered into that experiment, she'd had only the best interests of every teenager in Carson in mind. Though the teenager had fought her, she'd done everything she could to make Shannon see that getting pregnant at her age would be the biggest mistake she could ever make.

Then Asa put in his two cents, and that had pushed Luc past the point of endurance. He had no desire to work for an underhanded creep like Asa, even if it meant relocating and leaving behind everything and everyone he'd come to care so much about.

Suddenly the loud muffler on a passing car roused him from his thoughtful daze. After checking his watch, he realized that he'd been sitting outside his house for more than a half an hour rehashing what had taken place at the meeting. Slowly, he climbed from his car and made his way up the front walk and into the house.

As he walked into the living room, his footsteps echoed hollowly on the hardwood floor, reinforcing the emptiness of the building. Was this what his life would be like from now on? No one to share meals with. No one to talk to about his day. No one to love and be loved by. If all his future held was a solitary existence and a house that didn't come close to resembling a home, then it wouldn't make any difference if he lived in a penthouse or a tent.

Luc flopped down on the couch and stared blindly at the walls around him. He tried to ignore the pile of packing boxes he'd gotten from Keller's market, brought home and stacked in the corner . . . just in case. The empty cardboard boxes just underlined the bleakness filling him.

Already he missed the family-like dinners he'd shared with Mandy and Shannon, the laughter, the games and even the fights. Those few days had been the closest thing to having a real family that he'd ever known.

But most of all, his heart ached with missing Mandy. It amazed him that she'd come to mean so very much to him in such a short time. But she had, and now he'd lost her.

He'd been so wrong, so afraid if he loved her that any relationship they'd formed would end up in ruins like his parents' relationship. For Luc, the words *marriage* and *love* had always been synonymous with heartache and failure. And Mandy wanted nothing less than a committed relationship — love, security, babies — the only things, given the example set for him by his parents' marriage, he didn't think he'd been prepared to give her. But Mandy wasn't his mother, and he'd been stupid not to see that when he had a chance to tell her how he felt. And now, he'd never get that chance.

Tired of feeling sorry for himself, Luc decided it was time to tackle the task he'd been putting off for days. He dragged his body off the couch, grabbed the pile of newspapers stacked on the ottoman and began wrapping the pictures and knick-knacks he'd accumulated over the past three years and putting them in a box across the side of which he'd scrawled LIVING ROOM in black marker. He might as well be ready to move when the time comes. Besides, he needed something to keep his mind off Mandy.

He'd been at it for about an hour when a

knock sounded on his door. Laying aside a sheet of newsprint and wiping his soiled hands on a rag, he went to the door and swung it open.

Granny Jo Hawks grinned back at him.

"Granny Jo!" A cold chill raced down his spine. Granny had never come to his house before. "Is everything okay? Mandy?"

"Mandy's fine. Everything is fine." She glanced over his shoulder at the disarray in the living room. "But it doesn't appear as though everything's fine in there. Going somewhere?"

He laughed without humor. "In case you've forgotten, I just quit my job, and since there aren't any openings left for a principal in Carson, I'm going to have to be moving on." He glanced at the boxes and back at her. "No sense in putting off the inevitable."

"There's no need for you to be going anywhere." Granny Jo made an impatient sound. "Aside from being a mite on the impulsive side, your manners appear to need attention."

He frowned. "Excuse me?"

She nodded her head toward the living room. "Are you gonna leave me out here or invite me in?"

"I'm sorry. Please." He stood aside and

made room for her to enter. "My apologies."

She patted his shoulder and walked inside. "No need to apologize. You've had a rough day."

He laughed again. This time ironic humor colored his voice. "You might say that." He motioned toward the sofa. "Please, have a seat." Once she was seated, he joined her. "You still haven't told me what you're doing here."

"Well," she said, folding her hands in her lap, "the school board asked me to come talk to you. It seems they have one small problem."

CHAPTER 18

Another problem was not something Luc needed right now. He'd had more than his share today. With a tired sigh, he leaned back on the sofa and waited for Granny Jo to explain.

She pushed a stray lock of snowy hair off her forehead and cleared her throat. "I'm afraid the board voted Asa out as superintendent."

Tamping down the overwhelming urge to jump to his feet and cheer, Luc snickered. "And that's what you consider a problem?"

She didn't answer right away. In fact, she seemed hesitant, which wasn't at all like Granny Jo. When she had something to say, she usually said it, and anyone who didn't like it be damned. Then he detected a hint of a smile hovering on her lips. While he continued to stare at her, the smile grew until her grin spread ear to ear.

"No, that's not the problem. They voted

in a tentative replacement for him within a couple of minutes."

"Oh?" Now, his interested was piqued. "Who?"

Again she hesitated for a fraction of a moment. "You. That is, if you want the job." Before Luc could recover from the shock of her announcement and say anything, she went on. "That's what they sent me here for . . . to see if you'd take it." She laid her hand on his arm. "So, what do you say? Do you want to be Carson's School Superintendent?"

Luc remained speechless. Him? After what had happened in the board meeting, after they knew he'd entered into that agreement with Asa, they still wanted him? But did he want the job? Did he want to lose that hands-on connection with the kids? One of the things he enjoyed most about his work was being able to interact with the students, to help guide their path through education and aim them in the right career direction. Could he give that up? Did he *want* to give that up?

On the other hand, this would be a chance to stay in Carson, keep his home, remain where he had made friends, settle his roots even deeper into a community he loved . . . and see Mandy often, maybe too often.

Maybe with some other man.

It felt as though an invisible hand had reached into his chest and twisted his heart into painful knots. He could never stand seeing her with someone else. Never stand the idea of her lying in someone else's arms, having someone else's babies.

No matter how much it hurt, he had to admit that he had no one but himself to blame. Certainly not Mandy. The way things had come down, if the shoe was on the other foot, his trust in her would have been severely damaged, too. Just when he realized having a family was something he truly wanted, he'd screwed it all up by not being straight with the woman he loved. And even though he was almost certain he'd seen love in Mandy's eyes, he alone had made that fade.

"Luc?"

Granny's voice drew him from his guilty miasma. He blinked, wondering how long she'd been talking to him. "I'm sorry. I was thinking."

"I was saying, if you decide you don't want this position, the board is willing to renew your contract as principal of Carson High." Granny Jo's voice was tinged heavily with understanding, almost as if she could read his thoughts. "That would mean you could remain in Carson."

He shrugged and leaned back against the sofa. "Given the choice, I'd prefer the principal's job."

"Fine. Then it's settled. I'll let Catherine know." She started to get up, but he stopped her with a hand on her arm.

"But I don't want either job." Lord, but those words felt like they'd been cut from his gut.

Granny Jo looked stricken. "But —"

He shook his head. "There's no point in discussing it. I won't change my mind. It's time for me to move on." He hoped he'd managed to cover up the pain sitting in his gut like a large burning ball. Everything he'd ever dreamed of all his life was here. He had a home and friends and a love for this small town that was indescribable. It had taken him a while to realize it, but without Mandy, none of the rest mattered. "Things have changed. I've changed. I would love to stay here, more than anything, but I just — I can't." Remaining here in Carson and watching Mandy find happiness without him would just be too painful.

The school board would give him a good letter of recommendation now that Asa was gone. So there was no reason he couldn't start over somewhere else. Hadn't he spent the better part of his life doing just that? The difference was this time he'd do it with a broken heart.

Mandy watched Granny Jo climb back into her car and pull away from Luc's house. Still, she made no attempt to get out and go to his front door. Instead, she continued to stare at Granny's car. Even after it turned the corner she didn't remove her gaze from the empty street.

She'd come here with the full intentions of asking for Luc's forgiveness for misjudging him and to thank him for defending her against Laureene's insinuations. But when she'd arrived and saw Granny Jo go into the house, she'd decided to wait. Bad enough she had to eat her words. She had no desire to do it with an audience.

Now that Luc was alone, she no longer had an excuse to procrastinate. But she continued to do so. A tap on her driver's side window startled her. She jumped and turned to see Luc smiling down at her. She clutched her stomach to still the crazy flip-flops turning it every which way as though she were on some crazy amusement park ride.

"Did you plan on just sitting here all day, or are you going to get out?" he said through the small opening at the top of the window she'd made earlier for fresh air.

"How did you know I was here?"

"When I saw Granny Jo out, I spotted your car. You were so busy woolgathering you didn't see me approach." Busted. Heat rose up in her face. "So, are you going to get out?"

Her cheeks grew even warmer. Having been caught in the act, so to speak, she had little choice. "Yes."

He stepped back, opened her car door and waited while she climbed out. "How long have you been here?"

"Just a few minutes. In fact, I pulled in just as Granny left." A small lie, but one that prevented further embarrassment for her. He didn't need to know she'd been camped in front of his house for the last hour and a half.

He took her elbow, and small shock waves skittered up her arm. "Come on in, and I'll make us some coffee. I needed an excuse to avoid packing."

Packing? Why was he packing? Was he leaving after all? She'd presumed from the talk at the end of the board meeting that Granny Jo had come to offer him either his old job back or that of the superintendent. Maybe she'd wrongly assumed that he'd

276

jump at the opportunity to stay on in Carson.

Maybe he just wanted to get away from her.

Now, wait a minute! You have no reason to think that.

Luc had neither said nor done anything to suggest that she was the reason he was leaving . . . if he was leaving. How presumptuous it was of her to think she held that kind of importance in his life. She'd seen no proof that he was leaving, and until she did, she had to harness her imagination.

I'm reading too much into this. Hadn't he told me once that this house was the only real home he'd ever known? So why would he leave it now that he'd been offered his job back? Maybe he was just clearing away some unwanted items.

But when she stepped into the barren living room, her heart sank. Aside from the few pieces of furniture, nothing else remained in the room. A pile of boxes had been stacked neatly to the side, each marked *LIVING ROOM* in black marker. He was leaving. She had her proof right before her eyes. No one cleared an entire room of their belongings if they weren't planning on moving out.

"You *are* packing." She waved at the stack

of boxes waiting to be filled. "Why?"

For a moment, he stared at the boxes as if not understanding, and then he shrugged. "Well, since I won't be working in Carson anymore, getting started on this seemed the smart thing to do. But —" He didn't finished, just shook his head and motioned for her to precede him into the other room. "Let's get that coffee."

She followed, but she was still confused. "What about your job? The board said they'd take you back as principal or give you the super's job."

"I turned them down."

"But why?"

For a moment, he looked as if he was going to answer, but instead, he guided her into the kitchen.

She looked around. Evidently he'd just started packing up his belongings since the kitchen didn't look like it had been touched yet. Mandy took a seat in the breakfast nook.

"So what brings you here?" Luc set two cups of coffee on the table and then joined her.

He didn't offer her an answer to her question, or cream or sugar, and for some crazy reason, the latter warmed her a bit to know he'd remembered how she drank her coffee.

It was a tiny lifeline, but nevertheless something to cling to and fortify her nerves. As for the answer to her question, she knew Luc well enough to know that pressing him for information he didn't want to share was futile, so she let it drop . . . for now.

Mandy cleared her throat, but kept her gaze on the brown, steamy liquid in her cup. "I came to say . . . I'm really sorry that I misjudged you. It was wrong of me to jump to conclusions without waiting for an explanation."

Luc heaved a sigh that sounded a lot like one of relief. "I guess we both were a bit hasty. I was to blame, too. I should have told you at the start about Asa. At the very least, I should have talked to you about it when Catherine told you, instead of clamming up and assuming you wouldn't believe me."

Mandy raised her gaze to meet his. He was smiling, and she couldn't help but smile back. A sudden rush of warmth washed over her. Maybe things weren't as bad as she thought. Maybe —

"So we're friends again?" He sounded like a little boy hoping for forgiveness for some trouble he'd gotten into.

"Yes. Friends." But she wanted more . . . much more.

"Mandy, I need to tell you that. . . . Well, I've missed you."

"I've missed you, too."

He attempted to take her hand, but she folded them together in her lap. If he touched her, she'd never get through this.

As if sensing the invisible wall she'd erected around herself, he leaned away. "I've been thinking about my views on marriage, and, well . . . I was wrong to judge all relationships by my mom's and dad's or the people I knew in the military. I saw lots of good marriages with years of happiness behind them and ahead of them, too, but I guess, because of my parents' situation, I focused in on the bad ones."

Mandy held her breath and waited.

"I've always wanted a permanent home with roots in the community and friends that I wouldn't have to leave after a few months, and I have that . . . had that. But after the time we spent together at the lake, I realized I'm missing one of the most important things. I want someone to share it with . . . a family. Without that, the rest means nothing." He gazed deep into her eyes. "I've lived most of my life without one, and it's a lonely existence. Very lonely."

Mandy raised her gaze to meet his, her hands still clenched tightly in her lap. "I know. I've lived like that, too, Luc, or have you forgotten that?"

Shaking his head, he reached for her hand. She pulled back, and then dropped her gaze to her lap to avoid the hurt reflecting from his eyes. "No, I haven't forgotten. But neither have you, and that's why I want you to help me create that family. I didn't have a reason to accept the board's offer of a job, but I will have one if you'll marry me. Mandy, I want to stay in Carson, and I want you to be my wife."

Though her heart triple-timed, and her breath felt as though it were trapped in her chest, Mandy remained silent.

"Marry me, Mandy."

And she still waited . . . waited for *the* words she so longed to hear from Luc. Without those words, marriage would be empty and meaningless. Without those words, she could never say yes. Without them, she'd be entering into the same loveless existence her mother had endured.

Still, she waited, praying for the three words that were more important for her to hear than even the marriage proposal. But they never came.

He squeezed her hand. "Well, will you marry me?"

Slowly, her heart torn to shreds, disappointment clogging her throat, she pulled her hand away and stood. "No." That one word had taken every ounce of her will-power to utter.

Through the tears gathering in her eyes, she took one last look at the man she loved and then walked from the room.

"Mandy!" Luc had followed her and grabbed her arm to prevent her leaving. "I thought. . . . I thought you loved me. Was I wrong?"

More tears filled her eyes and spilled over onto her face. The aftereffects of so much pain and disappointment blocked her ability to speak. She so wanted to say yes to his proposal, but without his love, she couldn't.

Finally, she managed to squeeze the words out. "No, you weren't wrong. I do love you. I think I started loving you the day you went with me to see Alyce, and you offered to help her get her GED. I saw something good and honorable in you, something that told me I could trust you."

He frowned. "Then why won't you marry me?"

The tears ran unchecked down her cheeks. "Because . . . because you . . . don't love . . . me." The silent tears turned to sobs.

"What? Of course I love you."

She blinked back the tears. Joy unlike

she'd ever known filled her heart. "But you didn't say that. You said you wanted to marry me just so you could have a home and everything." She hiccupped.

Luc laughed and pulled her into his arms. "Silly girl. I want a *home and everything,* but only if you share it with me. I want to spend my senior years sitting in front of a fireplace and looking over to see you across from me playing with our grandchildren." He put her away from him and looked into her eyes. "I'm sorry I never said the words. I guess I figured that if I asked you to marry me, you'd know I loved you."

Mandy stood on tiptoe and kissed him long and hard. "Sometimes, a girl needs to hear it."

He grinned and kissed her back. "I'll make sure I remember that and tell you every day from now on."

This time, she kissed him. She curled her arms around his neck and pulled his mouth down hard on hers. The joining transmitted all the pent up longing that had hovered beneath the surface for so many days. All the wanting and needing. All the times she'd looked at him and wondered how it would feel to be in his arms because he loved her and not just because he desired her.

Luc pulled back, gasping for breath. "You

are playing with fire, Ms. James."

She grinned mischievously. "I know."

A twinkle glittered in his eyes. "Well, being the gentleman I am, I can hardly turn you away, now can I?" Then he grew serious. "Are you sure about this?"

She kissed him again, this time not letting him go until she couldn't stand the need building in her any longer. Taking a deep breath, she smiled up at him and whispered, "As sure as the sunrise over Hawks Mountain."

He scooped her into his arms and walked toward his bedroom. "What do you say we get started on that family?"

Mandy snuggled her face into the warm curve of his throat. "Sounds like a plan to me."

CHAPTER 19

The silky wedding gown had grown cold against her skin, so Mandy tucked her coat more securely around her and gazed out on the frozen surface of Lake Hope sparkling in the winter sunlight. An early snowfall had turned the entire landscape before her into a scene straight off a Christmas card. At times like this Mandy wished she could paint and preserve the memory on canvas. Unfortunately, she didn't have an artistic bone in her body.

She laughed and took great joy in the sound. It hadn't been all that long ago that genuine laughter had been missing from her existence. Had it only been a couple of months since she'd been sure she'd lost Luc, and her life had ended? Little did she know back then that it had just begun.

Mandy had come to Carson determined to make a difference in the lives of the teenagers in the town, and thanks to Catherine Daniels she had. The Carson High School Family Planning classes now included the baby simulators, and from all the preliminary reports, all was proceeding as expected. Catherine reported just yesterday that some of the teens had been rethinking their priorities.

But in accomplishing that, Mandy had changed her own life from one of a solitary existence to one filled with more happiness than she'd ever thought possible. She'd found love . . . real love . . . with a man she could lean on and trust to always be there for her, and she and Luc had made his lovely little house into a cozy home they would fill with love and laughter.

And soon —

Her thoughts were interrupted by two strong arms encircling her body from behind. "Shouldn't you come inside? It's cold out here." Luc's warm breath fanned the side of her chilled face.

"Not anymore." She smiled and snuggled into the haven of his body, enjoying the security it always offered her.

"I don't want you to catch cold." He slid his hand over her stomach. "Either one of you." He kissed her neck just below her ear, and pleasant chills coursed up her spine.

Mandy turned in his arms and cupped his

face. "We're both fine. I promise." She pressed her mouth to his. Her entire body awakened. She pressed closer.

They'd kept her pregnancy a secret. Not because conception had happened before marriage, but because they both wanted to bask in the miracle of their baby for a while before they shared the news.

He pulled away and grinned. "You're a brazen hussy, Mrs. Michaels."

"And you love it," she countered, enjoying the banter they often engaged in.

"Yup, every second of it." His grin widened, and he kissed her as if his life depended on it, and then released her lips. He studied her for a moment. "Are you sorry we had a bigger wedding than you wanted?"

Mandy recalled struggling with him about his desire for her to wear a white gown, not to mention the flowers and the caterer, but she'd finally given in when he explained that he wanted their wedding to be something she could look back on in the years to come. Something she could smile about and relive through the photos he'd taken. But mostly, she'd caved because he'd already given her more than she'd ever dreamed she could have, and this concession seemed to mean so much to him.

She shook her head. "No. I'm glad we had

all our friends here to share it with us." A breeze blew in off the lake, chilling the silk material of her wedding gown and in turn, stealing the warmth from her skin where the material touched it. Mandy shivered. "I guess it is a little colder out here than I thought. I could use a drink of something warm. I'll even settle for that poor excuse for coffee the doctor makes me drink."

"Decaf isn't all that bad, once you acquire a taste for it." He pulled her against him and guided her toward the French doors.

"And exactly how long will that take? I only have a little less than eight months, you know."

Luc slid the large glass door open and stepped back to allow her to enter the noisy room. As they stepped into the crowded reception Catherine had insisted on throwing to celebrate their wedding and Luc's reinstatement as principal of Carson High School, Becky Hart, her maid of honor, approached them.

"I've been looking all over for you." She looped her arm in Mandy's and began pulling her toward the hallway. "I have another wedding present for you."

"But you've already given us your gift." She and Nick had given them a full set of monogrammed, Irish table linens. "What else could there be?"

Becky smiled mysteriously. "You'll see."

As Mandy made her way across the floor of the large living room, she glanced around at the people who had come to mean so much to her and Luc, as well as people with whom she had only just become acquainted.

Granny Jo winked at her and cuddled Lili, her great, great niece, closer to her shoulder. Davy Collins devoured a piece of chocolate cake, while keeping a sharp eye on the window, beyond which a large, gray wolf waited patiently for him on the porch. Lydia, Davy's mom, was talking to a tall, handsome man that Mandy had been told was Ken Mackenzie, the brother of the town vet, Hunter Mackenzie. Hunter and Rose had been invited, but their twin baby girls had colds, and they'd opted to stay home. To Ken and Lydia's right, Jonathan Prince, a newcomer to Carson, and the owner of the fine mansion that had just been built outside of town, was deep in conversation with Catherine Daniels.

Gathered around the punch bowl, Mandy's bridesmaids, Shannon and Alyce, talked animatedly to Luc's best man, Nick Hart. Since Mandy and Luc started seeing each other, Nick and Luc had become fast friends due to their shared passion for baseball, and Luc had been adamant about asking Nick to stand up with him. Alyce was no doubt picking Nick's brain for her term paper on life as a military corpsman.

As Mandy took in the roomful of people, she marveled for the hundredth time at how full her life had become.

Becky urged her from her musings. "Come on."

She tugged on Mandy to get her to move faster, obviously very excited about her mysterious surprise. Then, when they'd made it into the hall, Becky stepped away from Mandy, leaned toward Luc and whispered something in his ear.

His eyebrows arched. "Really?" Becky nodded. "Okay." He kissed Mandy's cheek. "Be right back." Then he disappeared into the crowd.

Mandy came to an abrupt halt. "Okay, Becky, fess up. What's going on?"

Her boss grinned and shook her head. "You can stop asking because I'm not telling." Once more she began propelling Mandy toward the den at the back of the big house.

When they entered the den, the room was empty. As she glanced around the room, Mandy saw nothing that she would categorize as a surprise. Everything looked exactly the same. She sent Becky a questioning glare.

Becky sighed. "Lord, but you're impatient." She moved to the door that went into the kitchen, opened it and beckoned to someone Mandy couldn't see. "Please, come in."

The woman who entered the room was perhaps in her late forties or early fifties. Dressed casually in a navy dress, her earlobe-length, brown hair showed signs of graying, and her figure, while not plump, couldn't be classified slender either. She smiled at Mandy.

Mandy had seen that smile before. Did she know this woman? Mandy searched her memory.

"Hello." The woman extended her hand.

As Mandy reached for it, Becky said, "This is Helen Anderson."

Still at a loss as to who this person was, Mandy returned her smile. "Hello, Helen. Nice to meet you." Though she couldn't figure out why this stranger was at their wedding reception. She glanced at Becky, who just grinned. Obviously she wasn't ready to explain.

Before Helen could speak, the den door opened, and Luc ushered Catherine Daniels into the room. Becky took her hand and led her to within a few feet of the woman. "Catherine, this is Helen Anderson. She's a bit older than she was the last time you saw her, but you probably remember her as Hope."

Catherine gasped. Her face paled. Her hand flew to cover her heart. Tears filled her eyes. "My Hope?" she finally whispered.

Becky nodded, and Mandy collapsed onto the sofa. She couldn't believe that Catherine was finally getting to meet the daughter she'd last seen as an infant.

"How?" Catherine muttered, never moving her gaze from the woman standing silently before her, a faint smile curving her lips, moisture filling her eyes.

"You can thank Mandy. She insisted we find her for you." Becky's soft words cut through the emotion-filled silence.

Catherine remained frozen, oblivious to everyone and any conversation going on around her. She had eyes only for the child she thought never to see again.

Mandy swallowed the lump that had formed in her throat. She glanced at Luc and extended her hand to him. As his warm fingers closed around hers, she looked back at the two women facing each other.

"Momma?" Helen spoke for the first time. She extended her open arms toward Catherine. With a sob, Catherine walked into them.

Luc caught Mandy's and Becky's eye and motioned them toward the door. They all left, but not without Mandy glancing back at the mother and daughter reunion. A feeling she couldn't describe, a mixture of happiness that they'd finally found each other, and sadness that it had taken all this time, brought fresh tears to her eyes.

Luc put his arm around her and drew her to him. "You're a good woman, Mrs. Michaels. I love you, and, just as I promised, I plan on telling you that every day for the rest of my life."

Mandy caressed his cheek with her fingertips. She'd never tire of hearing him say those words. "I love you, too." She began walking back into the party arm-in-arm with him and then stopped. Looking up at this man whom she knew with all the certainty in her heart would never leave her side, she smiled contentedly. "Your father was wrong, you know."

"Oh? About what?"

She stood on tiptoe and kissed her husband. "Some things are forever."

Granny Jo's Journal

End of Fall

Hard to believe that Thanksgiving is just around the corner, and Christmas is right on its heels. Seems like just yesterday that my spring crocuses were pushing through the snow. I guess, when you get to be my age, time has wings on its feet.

Alyce's little Lili's sitting up all by herself now and jabbering away to beat the band. I can't understand a thing she says, but that doesn't seem to stop her. I finally talked Alyce into moving in with me until she gets her schooling done with. She passed her GED with flying colors, thanks to Luc Michaels, got herself a scholarship and is going to school in Charleston to become an LPN. I couldn't be prouder of her. Too bad her daddy can't see what a fine woman she's become. The darn fool is missing out on some of the best things in life because of his stubborn snobbishness.

Speaking of babies, I'm gonna be a great grandma come spring. Becky and Nick are expecting. Next week she'll find out if it's gonna be a boy or a girl. Nick says he doesn't want to know. Wants it to be a surprise. Becky says it's just practical to know so she can decorate the nursery in the right colors. Me? I just hope the little tyke has all the fingers and toes and everything else the good Lord intended.

Catherine Daniels had asked me to go with her to see that Jonathan Prince fella who just built that big house outside of town. I'm on a committee with her to raise money for an abused women's shelter here in Carson. Seems, since Becky and Mandy found Catherine's girl for her, she feels obligated to pay them back, and the shelter is Mandy's and Becky's pet project. They've been trying to figure out how to raise money to build it. Catherine came up with the idea of a fundraiser. Jonathan Prince has agreed to fund it for them. Nice man, that Mr. Prince. I plan on telling him just that when I go out there to give his aunt quilting lessons.

Mandy and Luc are building an addition on their house. They said they just need more room for Luc's home office. But a nursery's my guess. Now, they haven't officially announced anything yet, but I've been around long enough to know that when a woman gets that glow about her, there's only one reason for it . . . motherhood.

Come spring, there's gonna be a lot of new young'uns around Carson. Aside from all the human babies, Davy's Sadie is gonna have puppies. He's not sure if she found a male wolf or if Hank's German Shepard did the deed. Davy's over the moon at the idea of having a litter of puppies to care for. Lydia hasn't quite decided if this is a good thing or not. I'm sure she'll come around. Little ones — puppies or babies — are impossible to resist.

Well, Lili's fussing. Must have woke up from her nap. I'll have to run, but you all need to stick around. Christmas is coming, and here in Carson, aside from the beautiful decorations in the town square, the Christmas carols blasting from the speakers at Keeler's Supermarket and the smell of pine in the air, Christmas around here tends to be a magical time when anything can happen . . . and often does.

Merry Christmas and a Happy, Healthy and Prosperous New Year!

Much love,
Granny Jo

ACKNOWLEDGEMENTS

Thanks to Dolores Wilson and Vickie King, both West Virginia natives, who helped me keep the descriptions of their beautiful state accurate.

And to my great editor, Deb Smith, for her guidance, and Deb Dixon for my gorgeous cover.

ABOUT THE AUTHOR

Elizabeth Sinclair is the award-winning, bestselling author of numerous romance novels and two acclaimed instructional books for writers. Her novels have been translated into seven languages and are sold in seventeen countries. She lives in St. Augustine, Florida, with her husband and two dogs. Elizabeth is the mother of three children and "brags constantly" about her grandchildren.

Visit her at ElizabethSinclair.com

The employees of Thorndike Press hope you have enjoyed this Large Print book. All our Thorndike, Wheeler, and Kennebec Large Print titles are designed for easy reading, and all our books are made to last. Other Thorndike Press Large Print books are available at your library, through selected bookstores, or directly from us.

For information about titles, please call:
(800) 223-1244

or visit our Web site at:
http://gale.cengage.com/thorndike

To share your comments, please write:
Publisher
Thorndike Press
10 Water St., Suite 310
Waterville, ME 04901